Despair, Murder & Tragedy

21 Real Stories That Will Chill You to the Bone

Viv Hathaway

© COPYRIGHT 2023 VIV HATHAWAY

All rights reserved. No part of this book may be reproduced in any form or by any electronic or mechanical means, including information storage and retrieval systems, without permission in writing from the publisher, except by a reviewer who may quote brief passages in a review.

INTRODUCTION 6

"SURVIVING THE SHADOWS: THE UNTHINKABLE ORDEAL OF MARY VINCENT" 7

"ZOMBIE AUSTIN: TWO FAMILIES SHATTERED" 19

"BETRAYED BONDS: THE TRAGIC DEMISE OF MISSY AVILA" 41

"TWISTED FATES: THE TRAGIC DISAPPEARANCE OF RACHEL BARBER" 57

"UNEARTHLY URGENCY: THE PUZZLING ENCOUNTER THAT SAVED A LIFE ON BULLION BEND" 76

"DARK DEEDS UNVEILED: THE UNTHINKABLE BETRAYAL OF A FATHER'S TRUST" 83

"A TALE OF TWO LIVES: THE TRAGIC COLLISION OF WHITNEY CERAK AND LAURA VAN RYN" 98

"TWISTED TRUTHS AND TRAGIC CONSEQUENCES: THE UNBELIEVABLE SAGA OF RYAN WALLER'S INTERROGATION" 113

"UNFATHOMABLE CAPTIVITY: THE CHILLING ABDUCTION OF JAYME CLOSS" 136

"PIGGY PALACE NIGHTMARE: THE DISTURBING CRIMES OF ROBERT PICKTON" 147

"BENEATH THE DEPTHS: THE TRAGIC TALE OF THE KURSK SUBMARINE" 159

"TWISTED JOURNEY: UNRAVELLING THE ENIGMA OF JULIAN AND CAROLYN'S ABDUCTION" 175

"SHATTERED INNOCENCE: UNMASKING THE DARKNESS BEHIND JESSIE BLODGETT'S TRAGIC END" 198

"SECRETS OF THE SILENT HIGHWAY: THE PUZZLING DISAPPEARANCE OF DEVIN WILLIAMS" 221

"THE DARK WATERS OF TRAGEDY: THE ROGERS FAMILY'S HORRIFYING FATE" 234

"LEAP OF COURAGE: A TALE OF SACRIFICE AND SURVIVAL" 245

"BENEATH THE SMILE: A TALE OF DECEIT, GRIEF, AND DEADLY SECRETS" 262

"THE SILENT MENACE: UNRAVELLING THE MYSTERY OF GLORIA RAMIREZ" 277

"DESCENT INTO TURBULENCE: THE ORDEAL OF FLIGHT 14" 290

"DARK WATERS: THE TRAGIC DISAPPEARANCE OF TOM AND JACKIE HAWKS" 302

"TRAPPED BENEATH: THE UNTHINKABLE ORDEAL OF THE POINTE-À-PIERRE DIVERS." 321

INTRODUCTION

Contained within the pages of this book are 21 genuine stories that have befallen real individuals. These are tales of murder, kidnapping, assault, and other unspeakable horrors, intertwined with bewildering tragedies that defy explanation.

Be forewarned, some of these accounts are not tailored for the faint-hearted. You may find them unsettling, and graphic in nature. Nevertheless, their significance perseveres. They stand as stark reminders of life's delicacy, urging us to grasp each day with an unwavering appreciation for its value.

"SURVIVING THE SHADOWS: THE UNTHINKABLE ORDEAL OF MARY VINCENT"

During the 1960s and 1970s, hitchhiking gained immense popularity among young people as a mode of transportation in the United States. Hitchhiking involved individuals seeking rides from strangers, with hitchhikers positioning themselves along bustling roads, extending their arm with a raised thumb—a universally recognized gesture indicating their desire for a lift. This practice, which appears highly perilous in today's context, involved willing motorists pulling over when spotting a hitchhiker and offering them a ride.

However, the concept of hitchhiking has evolved over time. In present times, getting into a stranger's car or a driver picking up an unfamiliar person by the roadside is viewed as extremely unsafe. In stark contrast, during the earlier era, such actions were considered perfectly normal and socially acceptable.

On September 29th, 1978, Mary Vincent, a 15-year-old girl, found herself standing by a highway just outside Modesto, California. This location wasn't far from San Francisco. Mary, a rebellious teenager, had fled her Las Vegas, Nevada home due to her parents' bitter divorce, seeking solace with her grandfather in Los Angeles, California. After a few days there, Mary's homesickness compelled her to return to her parents and family in Las Vegas. Alone in her grandfather's house, she embarked on a hitchhiking journey back home. Having successfully hitchhiked from Los Angeles to Modesto, California, she was now seeking another ride to continue her journey south.

Alongside two other youthful hitchhikers, they held signs reading "Going South," departing from the traditional thumb-raising gesture to explicitly convey their intended direction. As a light blue passenger van pulled over in response to their signs, Mary's companions remained while she approached the vehicle.

Mary walked up to the van, peering through the open window. She asked politely, "Could you give all three of us a ride? We're headed south." The driver surprised her with a stipulation, "I can only give you a ride, not the others." Perplexed, Mary examined the interior, wondering about the restriction. Despite her reservations, she pressed further to include her companions. The driver, however, remained firm, agreeing to transport only her.

Mary was conflicted, recognizing the oddness of the situation. Yet, driven by her intense desire to return home, she reluctantly chose to leave her friends behind, collected her belongings, and entered the van. As the door shut, the driver pulled back onto the road and resumed driving.

After hitting the road, Lawrence cast a glance at Mary and initiated a conversation. He introduced himself as Lawrence Singleton, a 50-year-old man. In response, Mary introduced herself, and they engaged in light conversation. Lawrence put Mary at ease quickly. His friendly and polite demeanor reminded her of her own grandfather, fostering a sense of comfort.

As the journey progressed, Mary began to feel tired much earlier than anticipated. So, she asked Lawrence if she could doze off while he continued to drive. Lawrence readily agreed, reassuring her that it was perfectly fine to rest. With that, Mary shifted her attention away from Lawrence, nestled herself into a more comfortable position on the seat, and soon found herself slipping into sleep.

Later on, when Mary woke up, she glanced out the window and sensed that something was amiss. It was clear to her that they were traveling in the wrong direction. Mary turned to Lawrence and expressed her concern about their course. Lawrence's response was apologetic, claiming that he had made a mistake and promising to rectify it. Although Lawrence attributed the detour to an error, Mary's intuition whispered otherwise. She suspected that this diversion was no accident, as they were significantly off course.

Despite her suspicions, Mary chose not to confront Lawrence at that moment. Instead, she opted to closely watch his actions as he maneuvered the vehicle to reverse their course and head back in the correct direction.

As they continued along the correct route, Mary remained on high alert. She was cautious not to reveal her unease to Lawrence, given her limited familiarity with him. Although he had initially put her at ease, Mary couldn't shake the uncertainty surrounding his intentions.

Their journey eventually led them to a section of highway that traversed a wooded area, sparsely populated with vehicles. At this point, Lawrence unexpectedly expressed the need to pull over and use the bathroom. Though hesitant, Mary agreed, her sense of caution urging her to be compliant. As Lawrence began to steer the vehicle off the highway, Mary happened to notice that one of her shoes was untied. A swift, instinctual thought crossed her mind: she might need to flee, and having her shoes properly tied would be crucial for that.

Recognizing the potential suspicion that awkwardly tying her shoe inside the cramped vehicle could raise, Mary decided on an alternative approach. Once they had safely pulled off the highway, she planned to discreetly exit the vehicle and attend to her untied shoe. This pause would not only allow her to tie her shoe inconspicuously but also provide a moment to prepare for a potential escape.

As Lawrence pulled over, he didn't choose the highway's shoulder but instead veered onto an access road leading into the forest. This action immediately triggered alarm bells in Mary's mind. Uncertain of how to react, she refrained from speaking to Lawrence, not wanting to draw attention to her unease. Instead, she contemplated her options and tried to gauge her next move.

After a few minutes, when they were deep within the forest and hidden from the main road, Lawrence brought the van to a stop, supposedly to relieve himself. This presented an opportunity for Mary. Anticipating the chance to tie her shoe outside the vehicle and prepare for any unforeseen events, she swiftly exited the van. But her plans took a nightmarish turn as a sudden, powerful blow struck her from behind, rendering her unconscious.

Regaining consciousness, Mary found herself lying in the van's back compartment. Her view outside the windows confirmed they were still within the forest. Her initial disorientation was replaced by the realization that her hands and feet were secured, rendering her immobilized. Lawrence reappeared, opening the van's back doors and advancing toward her. Fear and confusion gripped Mary as Lawrence launched a brutal assault. Overwhelmed and defenseless, Mary pleaded with him to stop, her anguished appeals echoing in the confined space.

Following hours of torment, Lawrence ceased the assault and retreated to the front seats to sleep. Mary's struggles to free herself proved futile due to the tight restraints. Amid her vulnerability, she contemplated her predicament, her uncertainty about Lawrence's intentions gnawing at her. Eventually, Lawrence awoke during the night, his actions shrouded in silence. He returned to the back of the van and unleashed another wave of brutality upon her.

Without uttering a single word to Mary, Lawrence exited the back of the van and settled into the driver's seat. The van left the forest, eventually merging onto the main road. Then, he turned onto another access road, leading them away from the view of onlookers. Deep within a remote canyon, he parked the van. Approaching the back, where Mary lay whimpering and pleading, Lawrence's relentless torment continued for hours.

As the sun began to rise, Lawrence halted his assault. Stepping out of the van, he faced Mary and undid her restraints. With tears in her eyes and battered beyond recognition, Mary softly implored him to set her free. Responding with cruel irony, Lawrence proclaimed, "You want to be set free? I'll set you free."

Returning to his van, he retrieved a hatchet from his toolbox. Marching back to where Mary lay, he seized her left arm with his left hand and raised the hatchet high above her. In an instant, he brought it down, severing her arm just below the elbow. The shock of the assault sent Mary sprawling to the ground, her severed limb at her side. Her desperate screams and pleas fell on deaf ears as Lawrence grabbed her right wrist, hatchet in hand. Defying the limits of horror, he swung the hatchet repeatedly, severing her right arm from her body after four agonizing blows.

Mary's anguished cries echoed in the air as her body lay in a pool of blood. Yet, Lawrence remained fixated on an unexpected snag – one of Mary's amputated hands had clung to his arm when he severed it. Nonchalantly attempting to remove the hand, he finally succeeded, only to turn and realize that Mary had fallen silent, her lifeless form lying amid the gruesome scene.

Returning the bloodied hatchet to the van, Lawrence calmly approached Mary and began dragging her about a hundred feet down the road. Adjacent to the van's location lay a culvert, an underground tunnel designed to channel water beneath roads. This specific culvert extended about 30 feet beneath the road surface, featuring steep drop-offs on either side. Ensuring his actions went unnoticed, Lawrence placed Mary's lifeless body upon the precipice, causing her to plummet onto the rocks below. Lawrence descended to the body, maneuvering her into the culvert before coldly declaring, "Now you're free."

Despite the odds stacked against her survival, Mary clung to life. Remarkably, she retained vivid recollections of the entire ordeal, her memory encompassing the harrowing amputations and her desperate fight to survive. With her broken ribs and mutilated arms, she feigned death, hoping to elude further harm.

Left alone, Mary grappled with the choice to stay put or attempt escape. Lying contorted in the culvert, she resisted the urge to sleep, aware that succumbing would seal her fate. Overcoming exhaustion and blood loss, she roused herself, struggling to find her way out of the culvert. Muddying her wounds to stem the bleeding, she crawled to the road, using the stumps of her arms for leverage. Bare, blood-covered, and in shock, she embarked on a desperate three-mile run along the highway.

Encounters with passing vehicles were marked by shock and reluctance to assist. A young couple eventually stopped, stunned by Mary's appearance yet willing to help. They rushed her to the hospital, where Mary remained for a month, providing authorities with a detailed account of her attacker, Lawrence Singleton. Her description facilitated the creation of an accurate composite sketch, ultimately leading to Lawrence's capture after a neighbor recognized him on the news. Convicted for his heinous act, he only received a 14-year prison sentence, the maximum allowed by law at the time.

The culmination of her testimony brought a chilling encounter. Passing by Lawrence outside the courthouse, Mary had an unsettling proximity to her tormentor. In a final act of malevolence, Lawrence whispered, "I will finish the job if it takes me the rest of my life."

Eight years later, Lawrence Singleton was granted parole due to his good behavior during imprisonment. This development understandably struck fear into Mary, who had since become a wife and mother of two sons. The prospect of Lawrence's release ignited concerns that he might return to exact vengeance. However, rather than targeting Mary, Lawrence's focus shifted a decade later to another woman. Roxanne Hayes, a 31-year-old mother of three, became his next victim, tragically losing her life.

During Roxanne's murder trial, Mary courageously took the stand to testify against Lawrence. Her testimony played a pivotal role in securing a death sentence for him. Yet, before the execution could be carried out, Lawrence's life was claimed by cancer while in prison in 2001. This news left Mary with a sense of injustice, feeling robbed of the closure she had hoped for. Nonetheless, her sons found relief in the knowledge of their mother's attacker's demise, offering a measure of solace amidst the pain.

The outrage stemming from Lawrence's premature release, coupled with the tragic outcome of his subsequent actions, spurred the creation of the Lawrence Singleton Bill. This legislative measure empowered judges to impose 25-year to life sentences in cases involving acts of torture. Under this bill, Lawrence's heinous actions against Mary would have warranted a sentence that ensured he remained incarcerated for the rest of his life, preventing the tragedy that unfolded in the wake of his parole.

"ZOMBIE AUSTIN: TWO FAMILIES SHATTERED"

Austin Harris was born on December 21, 1996, to a dentist and a pharmacist. Their family resided in a picturesque home located in Palm Beach County, Florida. This area is renowned not only for being one of the most attractive and affluent places to live in Florida but also stands out as one of the most opulent locations in the entire United States. As of 2021, Palm Beach County boasts a remarkable 44 billionaires who have chosen to make this paradise their home.

In 2010, Austin's family life took an unexpected turn when his parents decided to part ways. Despite the shock, Austin and his younger sister Haley managed to adjust to their new family dynamics with relative ease. Their father moved nearby, ensuring their connection remained strong.

High school was Austin's platform to shine. He excelled in academics, consistently topping his advanced classes. While football and wrestling took center stage in his athletic pursuits, his imposing physique didn't match an aggressive demeanor. Despite football coaches' efforts to spark his aggression, Austin remained inherently mild and compassionate. After graduating in 2015, he received welcome news: acceptance into Florida State University's esteemed pre-med program.

College brought success, academic excellence, and a passion for bodybuilding that boosted his social media presence. However, beneath these accomplishments, he grappled with inner conflict. His journal chronicled a narrative of self-doubt, chronic insecurities, and challenges with fitting in. In a hidden struggle, he turned to drugs as a way to manage his emotions, exacerbating his internal battles.

During the summer, Austin's behavior took an unsettling turn. He moved his bed from his room to the garage, convinced that the house was haunted by demons at night. Rather than sleeping, he patrolled the house constantly, claiming to shield his family from these imagined demons. Every two hours, he'd loudly announce his mission while knocking on family members' bedroom doors. His family, baffled by his actions, suspected drug use as the cause. When they confronted him, he admitted to using various drugs—psychedelics, stimulants, and more. Consequently, his family focused on helping Austin overcome his drug use and regain stability.

Towards the end of the summer, Austin claimed to have stopped using drugs. However, his erratic behavior persisted. Around mid-August, the family decided to invoke the Baker Act. In Florida, the Baker Act allows individuals suspected of severe mental illness to be detained for up to 72 hours based on their loved ones' concerns. During this period, a comprehensive assessment is conducted to determine the individual's condition. At the end of the 72 hours, a treatment plan is formulated with the family's involvement.

However, before the family could utilize the Baker Act, something horrific happened.

On the morning of August 15th, one of Austin's very close friends, whom he had known since second grade, said Austin just showed up at his house without calling ahead of time or letting him know. This was very uncharacteristic. When this friend opened the door to see what Austin wanted, Austin just asked him, 'What year was I born?' The friend replied, 'Uh, 1996.' As soon as Austin heard this, he didn't react and simply turned around and left. The long-time friend watched Austin walking away, wondering what was going on. Was he high on drugs or drunk? The friend returned inside his house, pondering what he should do. After a couple of minutes, he decided he needed to call Austin and make sure he was okay. So, he called Austin. Although it's unclear what they talked about on the phone, the friend managed to convince Austin to come back to his house and spend the day together. In reality, the friend just wanted to ensure that Austin was okay.

Austin returned to his friend's house, and then the two of them left to meet up with some other friends who were in town for the summer, as well as Austin's sister.

The group decided to go to the beach for the day. During their walk to the beach, Austin told the group that he needed to get something from his house and that he would meet them down at the water. The group assumed Austin was fine and agreed to meet him there.

Austin went to his house, and when he returned to the beach and reunited with his friends, he had changed his outfit. He was now wearing a thick, large football jersey, long sweatpants that were also thick, two wristwatches, and sunglasses. As he walked onto the beach in this unusual attire, his friends commented on his strange outfit, joking around. However, Austin didn't find it funny at all. Initially quiet, he eventually lashed out and warned them that if they called him crazy, he would kill them. His friends realized he was serious and stopped teasing him. Despite this, Austin's agitation was evident.

His sister approached him, trying to calm him down and reassure him that everything was okay. During their conversation, Austin suddenly reverted to a more normal demeanor. He turned to his sister and said, 'I'm actually half-horse and immortal.' His sister was taken aback and said, 'What? You really need to get professional help. You should see a therapist or a psychologist. Something is wrong with you, and it's been wrong all summer. You need help now.' Astonishingly, Austin responded positively, acknowledging that there was indeed something wrong and that he needed help.

After this exchange, Austin and the rest of the group spent several more hours at the beach. In the evening, Austin, his sister, and Austin's close friend (the one who had seen Austin earlier in the day) all decided it was time to leave. They headed to Duffy's, a restaurant in town, where they were meeting up with Austin's father and his father's girlfriend.

As they were approaching the restaurant, walking along the sidewalk and nearing the entrance, Austin suddenly turned to his sister and said, 'Hey, I need to test out my immortality.' He turned away from her and the sidewalk, facing traffic, and started walking into the road as if he intended to let a car hit him to prove his immortality. Reacting swiftly, his sister managed to grab him and pull him back onto the sidewalk. She positioned herself on his left side and guided him along the sidewalk to the front door of the restaurant. There, the trio met up with Austin's father and his father's girlfriend. The five of them entered Duffy's restaurant. Inside, they were promptly seated at a booth in the back of the restaurant. A CCTV camera observed them during their time inside the building. The clock showed approximately 7:45 pm as they settled in.

Sitting at the booth, about three minutes after they sat down, Austin got up and walked away from the table, as if heading toward the bathroom. However, he suddenly stopped, turned around, and walked back towards the front of the building. He then walked out of the front doors, leaving the restaurant altogether. Just a minute later, Austin returned inside the restaurant and walked right back to his table, sitting down as if nothing had happened. Less than ten minutes later, Austin got up from his table again. This time, instead of pretending to go to the bathroom, he walked straight from his table out the front doors of the restaurant and disappeared.

A couple of minutes later, Austin's mother, who wasn't at dinner with them, was at her nearby home when she heard someone entering her house. She went to see who it was and found her son Austin in her kitchen, drinking vegetable oil. Parmesan cheese was scattered all over the counter, which he apparently had been eating as well. She rushed over and grabbed the vegetable oil, placing it back on the counter and telling him to stop. Austin complied and then went up to his room to change his clothes. His mother drove him back to the restaurant and watched him get out of the car, enter the restaurant, and then she drove away.

Around 30 minutes after he left for the second time, Austin walked through the front doors of the restaurant, now wearing a different shirt and hat. He walked to the back of the restaurant where his sister, friend, father, and father's girlfriend were sitting, and again he sat down as if nothing had ever happened. At first, it appeared that everyone at the table was silent, but then Austin's father clearly said something to him. The tone seemed somewhat hostile. As it turned out, Austin's father, who loved his son and was entirely at a loss for what to do with him. When Austin sat back down, his father asked, 'What is wrong with you?' In response, Austin stood up, pressed his father's face back against his seat, and pinned him there momentarily. Eventually, he let go, left the booth, and walked out of the restaurant for the third time.

Austin's friend, who was dining with them, got up and tried to follow Austin, but he was about 30 seconds behind. By the time he reached outside, he didn't know where Austin had gone, so he quickly returned to the restaurant. He informed the rest of the group that he didn't know Austin's whereabouts. At this point, they knew he was completely unstable and had no idea where he might go, and whether he might pose a threat to himself or others. Consequently, Austin's father would call the police and have them search for him.

About four miles away from the restaurant, Michelle Mishcon, a 53-year-old woman, was sitting in her garage, engrossed in watching TV. Typically, her husband, John Stevens, aged 59, would be there with her, but he was out walking their dog. In that moment, Michelle was alone. The couple had been married for nearly 20 years, each bringing three children from previous marriages. They were deeply in love, and their garage was akin to a joyful haven, essentially functioning as their living room. Their penchant for leaving the garage door wide open allowed them to greet neighbors, invite people over for drinks, or engage in casual conversations. Known as a happy and affectionate couple, they were a delight to be around. According to their children, they had both recently retired. John had concluded his tenure as the owner of a landscaping company, while Michelle had retired from her role as a financial advisor. The prospect of retirement was met with excitement, as they looked forward to spending more quality time together, relishing moments with friends, fishing on their boat with their dog, and simply lounging in their beloved garage.

Their neighbor across the street, Jeff Fisher, was in his middle age and had developed a close relationship with the couple. He often looked after their dogs when they were away and frequently joined them in their garage for drinks and companionship. On this particular evening, he was at his own house, retiring for the night. As he prepared to sleep, he became aware of unusual noises emanating from outside his window, in the vicinity of John and Michelle's property across the street. Intrigued, Jeff strained his ears to discern the source of the sounds. Suddenly, a blood-curdling scream, a woman's cry, shattered the stillness. Jeff sprang into action without hesitation. He leaped out of bed, rushed downstairs, and exited his front door, his attention directed towards Michelle and John's property. He observed an unfamiliar young man, slamming the door of Michelle's car, parked in her driveway. The young man started walking up the driveway toward the garage, where Michelle stood, visibly terrified. This young man was none other than Austin Harrouff.

While Jeff was uncertain of the precise situation unfolding, he was alarmed by the scream he had heard. As he gazed across the street, he witnessed a distressing scenario. Before he could cross the road to reach Michelle, he saw Austin grabbing her and forcefully throwing her to the ground. Austin then proceeded to assault her while atop her. Without hesitation, Jeff ran across his own property, endeavoring to reach Michelle and, if necessary, confront Austin. As he approached the driveway, he saw Austin abruptly disengage from Michelle, turning to face Jeff. Austin issued a warning to Jeff, saying, "You don't want a part of this." Undeterred, Jeff, who was quite a robust individual, assessed the situation and understood that Michelle was in grave danger. Without hesitation, he lunged towards Austin, who, in response, swung at Jeff and struck him across the side of his head. Though Jeff absorbed the blow and didn't lose his footing, he seized Austin by the collar, forcibly throwing him to the ground. Austin hit the pavement with force, landing face-first.

Jeff anticipated that Austin might not rise immediately. However, he suddenly felt an intense, searing pain on his face, head, neck, and back. Blood covered his arms, indicating that Austin had wielded a knife during the altercation. Jeff was struck across multiple points by the knife, resulting in five distinct puncture wounds from that single swing. In that moment, Jeff believed his injuries could be fatal, fearing that his jugular might have been compromised, and he was bleeding profusely. With Austin rising to his feet once more, knife in hand, Jeff's life was in jeopardy. He decided he had to flee. He sprinted onto Michelle's property, hoping to divert Austin's attention away from her, pounding on doors as he moved through the house. Exiting through a rear door, he circled the property, attempting to create distance. Eventually, he dashed across the street to his own home, not once glancing back to verify if Austin was pursuing him. Upon reaching his residence, he secured the door, and immediately contacted 911.

Jeff (heavy breathing): "Please, we need medical assistance urgently. There's a young man viciously beating up a woman across the street." Dispatcher: "Are either of them injured? Can you tell from where you are?" Jeff: "Yes, there's a girl laying on the ground. He beat her up. I ran over; I'm bleeding profusely from my injuries here at the moment." Dispatcher: "Okay." Jeff: "I'm not entirely sure what happened." Dispatcher: "Can you determine if the woman is conscious?" Jeff: "No, it doesn't seem like she is. I've been stabbed in my back and I'm bleeding pretty bad."

After the call was placed and Jeff was certain that help was on the way, he was barely conscious. All he could remember thinking was, "I hope this maniac has abandoned his attack and just run off, or I hope John has come outside and is helping his wife." Unfortunately, all Jeff could hear were the sounds of Austin across the street, emitting loud, animalistic grunting sounds. Simultaneously, the air was filled with the piercing screams of someone, but Jeff couldn't discern whether it was one person, two, male, or female. He was engulfed in a cacophony of screams and grunts

Moments later, the police arrived on the scene. The following account is provided by the second responding officer, who we'll refer to as Sam. The first responding officer will be referred to as Chloe. As Sam approached the scene, he raced down the street with sirens blaring, pulling up right behind Chloe's parked police car in front of John and Michelle's property. Chloe was already charging up the driveway, gun drawn, ready to engage whoever was there. Sam quickly exited his car, gripping his gun, and as he moved towards the driveway, his view was obscured by the presence of two parked cars. This obscured his line of sight to whatever was at the top of the driveway, where Chloe was poised with her gun. He rushed past the left side of the parked car, then he reached the top of the driveway and saw a disturbing sight.

A broad stream of blood, about six feet wide, painted the driveway red. Around the left side of the left car, he saw Chloe aiming her gun at something in front of her. Sam joined her on her left side, looking down the driveway. What lay before them was a man lying on the ground, his eyes open, staring up at Chloe and Sam. He was lying stiffly, his gaze fixed on them. This man was John Stevens, and atop him was Austin, positioned sideways on John's chest. Austin had his left arm coiled around John's neck, holding him in place. With his right arm, he was doing something to John's face, though Sam couldn't quite make out the details. What was evident was that there was an aggressor, and they needed to intervene promptly. Chloe was unable to take a shot, as firing her gun carried the risk of hitting John and potentially causing fatal harm. With urgency, Sam advised Chloe to wait for a moment. Positioned now on Chloe's right side,

Sam assessed the situation. Austin remained engrossed in his grisly activity, seemingly impervious to the presence of officers. They were practically invisible to him. Stepping around Chloe to her other side, Sam resolved to tase Austin. Positioned to the right of Chloe, he faced Austin's back, ready to deploy the taser.

As he prepared to shoot the taser, he caught sight of Austin's actions – he was inserting his hand into John's mouth, pulling at his cheek as if hooking a fish. Then came the shock – Austin bit into John's cheek, tearing off flesh and consuming it. A horrifying image that Sam could hardly believe. Reacting quickly, Sam shot the taser into Austin's back, but to no effect. Austin remained fixated on his gruesome task. Unperturbed, he continued to devour John's face. Sam ordered Chloe to step back momentarily. Austin's actions were beyond comprehension – he wasn't responding to the presence of law enforcement; he was lost in his macabre feast. Sam moved to Chloe's right side again, where he stood next to the car, facing Austin head-on. He aimed a powerful kick at Austin's face, knocking him off John's visage and onto the ground. As Austin lay momentarily stunned, Sam seized the opportunity. He leapt over John's body, landing on Austin's face, stunning him further. This provided Sam with the opportunity to apply handcuffs. With one handcuff secured, Austin resisted fiercely as Sam attempted to cuff his other wrist. Austin's deranged screams of "Kill me! I'm eating humans!" echoed, leaving Sam bewildered. The struggle persisted until additional officers arrived on the scene. After a concerted effort involving several officers, Austin was finally subdued and handcuffed. With Austin finally restrained, the officers attended to the victims. Tragically, Michelle had succumbed to her injuries and was pronounced dead at the scene. John, despite being alive when the police arrived, had succumbed to the multitude of injuries he had sustained – from stabbings to brutal beatings, and the horrifying act of having a portion of his face ripped off.

It is believed that after Jon returned from his walk, which would have been right after Jeff had been attacked and ran back to his house, Jon saw Austin in his garage attacking his wife. Jon immediately intervened in an attempt to save her. Tragically, Jon would lose his life while courageously trying to protect the woman he loved. Their dog, thankfully, survived the attack unharmed and was entrusted to one of their children for care. Jeff Fisher, the neighbor who bravely attempted to rescue Jon and Michelle, managed to survive the attack and eventually made a complete recovery.

After Austin was finally handcuffed and restrained on the driveway, he suddenly became unresponsive. He was promptly transported to the hospital, where it was determined that he had ingested poisonous chemicals, most likely from inside John and Michelle's garage. These chemicals were causing his organs to fail. Subsequently, Austin fell into a coma for 11 days due to the ingestion, but medical intervention managed to save his life. He eventually emerged from the coma and underwent a full physical recovery. Initially, it was assumed that Austin's history of drug abuse played a role in the violent crime he committed. Speculation arose that he might have been under the influence of drugs like bath salts or flakka—synthetic hallucinogens known for causing intense, aggressive behavior. These drugs were prevalent in Florida and had led to other individuals engaging in violent rampages. This notion seemed logical given the circumstances. However, when Austin's toxicology report was finally available, it showed only a minimal amount of THC, the compound found in marijuana, in his system. The other substances in his system were administered by medical professionals at the hospital, indicating that at the time of the attack, Austin was effectively sober. When the police questioned Austin about why he committed this heinous act, he initially responded with phrases like "I don't remember" and "I don't know." However, over time, he began to open up and share a story that appeared incomprehensible to any rational person.

According to his account, after leaving the restaurant where his family was, he claimed to have encountered a dark, evil figure with a white face. Feeling threatened, he ran away from this entity and ended up about four miles away in John and Michelle's neighborhood. He was drawn to a brightly lit garage, not intentionally, where he believed the occupants could aid him against this sinister figure. In the garage, Austin approached Michelle, seeking help in his frantic state. But his actions likely came across as erratic, causing Michelle to scream. At this point, Austin believed Michelle to be a witch and, driven by his delusion, attacked her with a knife. Following the attack, he consumed what he thought was a bottle of alcohol but was likely poisonous lawn chemicals found in the garage. Austin claimed that he then turned his attention toward the doorway of the garage, where he saw another figure with a dog—possibly John returning from his walk. He claimed his memory went blank at this point.

Despite public skepticism about his story—attributing it to a ploy to plead insanity for a reduced sentence—a renowned forensic psychologist named Philip Resnick conducted an extensive assessment of Austin's mental state. Resnick's 38-page report concluded that Austin was experiencing a severe psychotic episode during the attack. Austin's persistence in biting John's face even when faced with lethal threats and physical interventions indicated a loss of basic survival instincts. This behavior aligns with a phenomenon known as clinical lycanthropy delusions, in which an individual believes they are not human and often identifies as a werewolf or similar creature. Austin's prior claims of being half horse or half dog, as well as his animalistic actions during the attack, fit this pattern.

Resnick's assessment shed light on the fact that Austin was not engaging in a mere act to secure an insanity defense. Rather, his actions aligned with a severe psychotic episode that led him to genuinely believe he was acting as a creature of this nature.

After Austin emerged from his coma but before his transfer to jail, he agreed to be interviewed by clinical psychologist and TV personality, Dr. Phil McGraw. In their 10-minute Zoom interview, Austin broke down in tears and expressed profound remorse to the victims' family. He admitted he didn't fully comprehend why the incident occurred and acknowledged that something was fundamentally wrong with him, necessitating help. He fervently hoped that the victims' family could eventually find it in their hearts to forgive him. Nevertheless, it seems unlikely that the victims' family will extend forgiveness any time soon. They were hoping for him to receive the death penalty.

Austin Harrouff had his trial in February 2022 and was found guilty of two counts of first-degree murder and one count of attempted murder. He was sentenced to life in prison without the possibility of parole. However, Harrouff's lawyers appealed the verdict, arguing that he was not mentally competent to stand trial.

In November 2022, a Florida appeals court upheld the verdict but ordered a new trial because Harrouff's lawyers were not given enough time to prepare their case. Harrouff's new trial was scheduled to begin on November 8th, 2022, but was postponed on the morning of the trial date. Harrouff's lawyers entered a plea of not guilty by reason of insanity, and the judge accepted the plea. Harrouff was then committed to a secure mental facility until doctors and a judge agree that he is no longer dangerous. Currently, Austin Harrouff is being held at the Florida State Hospital in Chattahoochee, Florida. He will remain there until he is deemed no longer a danger to himself or others.

"BETRAYED BONDS: THE TRAGIC DEMISE OF MISSY AVILA"

In 1985, a group of hikers embarked on a journey through a vast forest in southern California. As they walked along a trail, one of them glimpsed through the trees to their side. There, they noticed a stream meandering alongside the very path they were on. Their attention was soon captured by an unusual sight within the stream. Intrigued and puzzled, the hikers veered away from the trail, descending towards the stream's course. The sight that awaited them prompted a collective pause, leading them to call the police.

In 1985, Michelle Avila, a 17-year-old known by her nickname "Missy," resided in the working-class town of Arleta, California, just north of Los Angeles. Despite her petite stature—

standing under five feet tall and weighing less than 95 pounds—Missy possessed a vibrant and magnetic presence. Coupled with her beauty and genuine kindness, she was immensely popular at her high school.

Nevertheless, her life wasn't devoid of challenges. A year prior, during her sophomore year, a false rumor had circulated throughout her high school, alleging that she had been involved with boys already in relationships. This rumor escalated into an attack on Missy by a group of girls, with Sonia Bonn taking a leading role. Charges were filed against Sonia, but the case faced delays and was set to go to court in October 1985, as Missy entered her junior year.

On October 1st, a week before her court appearance, Missy arrived home from school and informed her mother of her intention to spend the afternoon with friends. Irene, her mother, granted permission but reminded her to return by 6 pm. Shortly after, a friend named Laura Doyle arrived, and they departed together. However, by 6 pm, Missy had not returned home.

Laura, who had driven Missy that day,

grew increasingly concerned. She contacted Irene and explained that she had dropped Missy off after their hangout. However, Missy's absence persisted.

Laura recollected the events of the day Missy went missing how they had driven to Stonehurst Park, where Missy had spotted two unfamiliar guys near a blue Camaro. Laura had reservations about these strangers but allowed Missy to approach them. Missy's final words before stepping out were, "Okay, bye." Laura decided to leave the park to get gas, assuming Missy could take care of herself.

Upon Laura's return to the park, both Missy and the Camaro were gone. Laura continued searching for a while, but Missy remained untraceable. Laura called Missy's house, hoping she had made it home, only to be met with the news of Missy's absence. Distressed, both Laura and Irene launched a frantic search, reaching out to friends and acquaintances, yet finding no trace of Missy.

As the reality of Missy's disappearance sank in, Laura and Irene resolved to contact the police. Laura's recollection of the blue Camaro and the two strangers became vital information for investigators. Despite their best efforts, days passed without progress. Both professional and community searches yielded no leads on Missy's location or the identities of the two young men and their blue Camaro.

On October 4th, merely three days after her disappearance, the hikers discovered Missy. However, it took an additional three years for investigators to fully comprehend the events of that crucial day. Eventually, the testimony of a single eyewitness would reveal what had truly happened to Missy.

On Tuesday, October 1st, 1985, Missy returned home from school with plans to spend time with friends. Her mother set a curfew of 6 pm. Moments later, her friend Laura picked her up, and they drove off. They drove around town before arriving at Stonehurst Park. For context, Missy had two close friends: Laura Doyle and Karen Severson. The trio had a strong bond, but tensions had escalated a month earlier due to a rumor about Missy's involvement with boys in relationships, including Laura and Karen's boyfriends. That day, Missy, Laura, and Karen's meeting at the park was meant to mend their strained friendship. Karen and Missy had clashed due to the rumor, resulting in a physical altercation in which Karen slapped Missy, consequently over the next month they wouldn't be talking to each other.

However, on the morning of October 1st, Karen reached out to Missy, expressing regret for the fight. Missy, touched by the apology, was open to reconciling. Plans were made to meet at Stonehurst Park and revive their friendship.

Laura picked up Missy pulled their vehicles into the parking lot at Stonehurst and selected a spot to park. They patiently awaited the arrival of Karen, who showed up just minutes later. However, Karen's entrance marked the beginning of a chaotic scene. She arrived at the parking lot with great speed, screeching to a halt right alongside Laura's car. Karen's parking was so tight that Laura couldn't open her car door without hitting Karen's vehicle. In Karen's car, seated closest to Laura's, was Eva Chirumbolo, a 17-year-old friend of the girls. Karen had invited Eva over for dinner, but without any prior explanation, Karen had impulsively driven to Stonehurst and parked aggressively beside Laura's car.

Eva sat in the passenger seat, perplexed, glancing between Karen and Laura, unsure of the unfolding situation. Karen demanded that Eva roll down her window, prompting Eva to comply. Laura and Missy, utterly bewildered, observed the escalating confrontation. Laura rolled down her window after Eva, and then they could hear Karen's furious tirade. Karen directed a barrage of vile insults solely at Laura, ignoring Missy. It took Laura a moment to comprehend the situation fully, but once she did, she retaliated with her own barrage of insults. As Laura and Karen exchanged heated verbal volleys, Missy and Eva remained seated in their respective passenger seats, completely in the dark about the reasons behind the confrontation.

Suddenly, just as quickly as Karen had arrived and initiated the confrontation, she shifted her car back into drive and sped away from the parking lot. Laura, fueled by anger and frustration at the hurtful comments Karen had hurled at her, reacted swiftly. She started her car, shifted into drive, and sped out of the parking lot in pursuit of Karen. Over the next 45 minutes, Karen and Laura recklessly navigated through the city and into the mountains. Karen's driving was erratic, swerving from side to side as she sped along the desolate roads. Laura pursued closely, consumed by a surge of road rage.

Initially, both Missy and Eva attempted to reason with their respective drivers, urging them to halt the dangerous pursuit. They implored Laura and Karen to pull over, emphasizing that whatever conflict had caused this frenzy wasn't worth risking their lives over. Unbeknownst to Missy and Eva, there was a much deeper underlying issue between Laura and Karen that had fueled this intense chase.

Their pleas fell on deaf ears, and the adrenaline-fueled drive continued. After a nail-biting 45-minute journey, the road led them to a dirt parking lot within a vast forest. Karen came to a halt, narrowly avoiding a collision, and Laura managed to stop right beside her. The two drivers immediately exited their cars and confronted each other, their anger boiling over into physical shoving and shouted insults. Eva remained in the passenger seat, hoping for the situation to deescalate, while Missy, torn between her two best friends on the brink of violence, decided she needed to intervene.

Missy stepped out of her car, determined to separate Laura and Karen, who were locked in a confrontation that seemed ready to erupt at any moment.

As Missy reached for the car door, an unexpected shift occurred. The intense argument between Karen and Laura, which had been escalating just moments before, came to an abrupt halt as if a switch had been flipped. Their attention turned to Missy, ending their dispute. In a strangely synchronized manner, they hurried over and positioned themselves by Missy's passenger door, preventing her from closing it and effectively trapping her inside. With a menacing tone, Karen confronted Missy directly. She confessed that their entire conflict had been a sham – Karen and Laura were not truly at odds with each other; instead, their anger was aimed at Missy. With swift coordination, they pulled Missy out of the car and forcefully pinned her against the side of Laura's vehicle.

Laura and Karen cornered Missy,

accusing her of being involved with their boyfriends and claiming to have indisputable evidence of her actions. Overwhelmed by fear and anxiety, Missy attempted to deny the allegations, but the aggressive confrontation from Karen and Laura left her feeling powerless and unable to effectively defend hers

Taking advantage of Missy's vulnerability, Karen and Laura forcibly moved her away from the car and directed her toward the forest. Missy, who was significantly smaller than both Karen and Laura, couldn't offer resistance. Instead, she complied, shuffling along, with Karen and Laura intermittently pushing her forward. Eva had joined the group, trailing behind without active involvement.

After a few minutes, Karen and Laura successfully guided Missy to the entrance of a narrow trail that extended from the parking lot into the woods. Laura positioned herself in front of Missy, while Karen remained behind. With Missy sandwiched between them, the two commanded her to continue following them along the trail. Overwhelmed and fearful, Missy complied, walking in step behind

Laura and enduring Karen's occasional shoves. Eva continued to linger behind, still not intervening.

As the group ventured deeper into the woods, Laura abruptly halted, turning to face Missy. Missy looked up at Laura, only to be met with a sudden punch to the face. Before she could react, Karen joined in, and what had initially been a psychological confrontation escalated into a physical assault. Karen and Laura subjected Missy to a barrage of punches, kicks, and stomps, while Eva stood by as a passive observer.

The beating eventually ceased, but Laura and Karen's intentions were far from fulfilled. Laura produced a knife, she grabbed a hold of Missy's hair, beginning to hack it off. Missy cherished her hair, and Laura and Karen knew this vulnerability all too well. Laura continued the brutal act with her knife, while Karen, lacking a weapon, resorted to pulling Missy's hair out with her bare hands.

After a substantial portion of Missy's hair had been forcibly removed, Laura and Karen relented, momentarily stepping back. Missy, now curled into a fetal position, was left sobbing and broken. Yet, Laura and Karen were not finished. They proceeded to restrain Missy, securing her hands behind her back and gagging her mouth to stifle her cries. Throughout this traumatic ordeal, Eva remained on the periphery, still inactive.

With Missy now bound and gagged, Laura shifted her focus to a nearby stream situated just a short distance away.

Laura made her way down to the stream, wading in until the water reached about eight inches on her leg. With an unsettling intent, she gazed back up the hill at Missy, Karen, and Eva. While keeping her eyes locked on Missy, Laura reached down, allowing her fingers to skim through the water's surface. In a disturbing gesture, she beckoned Missy to join her in the water, taunting, "Why don't you come down and get in the water with me?" Missy hesitated, and in that moment, Karen sprang into action. With a forceful yank, she pulled Missy up and pushed her downhill. Hindered by her bound hands, Missy toppled forward, unable to shield herself, and rolled to a stop near the water's edge.

Before Missy could recover, Karen and

Laura descended upon her. They grabbed her shoulders and began dragging her toward the water. Meanwhile, Eva, who had been observing the unfolding horror, didn't intervene. Instead, she turned and fled down the trail back toward the cars. However, upon reaching the cars, she realized they were locked, and she was too far away from any help to walk. Reluctantly, she returned to the trail, heading back toward the stream where her friends were.

While heading back, Eva heard a horrifying scream that momentarily froze her in fear. She turned and ran back to the cars. She sat down between the vehicles, rocking back and forth in terror.

An hour later, Laura and Karen emerged from the trailhead, drenched but seemingly light-hearted. Missy was not with them. Unbeknownst to Eva, the true horrors that had unfolded were even worse than her fears.

When Missy had initially been pulled into the water, Laura and Karen had forced her onto her stomach in the shallow water. Despite her bound hands, she valiantly struggled to keep her head above the water's surface. Laura responded by tightly grasping Missy's legs and submerging them, as Karen exerted pressure on her head, pushing it downwards. The struggle intensified as Missy fought to breathe, periodically managing to lift her head above the water for a gulp of air before being forcibly pushed back under.

Missy's desperate fight continued until she released a piercing scream. This scream, a primal cry for help, marked a turning point. Karen and Laura adjusted their grip, shoving Missy's head back into the water. The struggle persisted, but Missy's energy waned.

Recognizing Missy's weakening state, Laura and Karen saw an opportunity. They momentarily released their hold on Missy and dashed to the side of the stream where a log lay. This log, weighing over a hundred pounds, was heavier than Missy. With grim determination, Laura and Karen lifted the log and carried it back into the stream. In a final act of brutality, they dropped the log directly on the back of missy's head, forcing it down into the water permanently.

Karen and Laura emerged from the

forest trail a few minutes later. Without a hint of remorse, they got into their cars, with Eva joining Laura. The trio then left the parking lot, leaving behind the lifeless body of their former friend. When her remains were discovered and the police arrived, they found unrelated items: cigarette butts, a beer bottle, and scattered men's overalls near the location where Missy was found. Despite the lack of connection to the crime, these items oddly contributed to a false narrative, hinting at the involvement of two men in a blue Camaro.

Laura's description of two "troublemaker" guys further fueled suspicions. The police doggedly pursued this lead, and the murder case eventually grew cold. It wasn't until three years after Missy's death that Eva, who had been coerced into silence by Karen and Laura, finally came forward. In a courageous move, she revealed to the authorities that it was Karen and Laura who had orchestrated Missy's murder.

The roots of this tragic event lay in jealousy and resentment that had festered over the years. As Missy flourished into a radiant young woman, Laura and Karen's feelings of inadequacy grew. They nurtured their jealousy, which gradually transformed into resentment and then pure hatred. In 1984, Karen and Laura initiated a false rumor about Missy's promiscuity, leading to a vicious attack on her. But this wasn't sufficient for them. A year later, in September 1985, they hatched a sinister plan to kill Missy.

Their scheme began with the circulation of yet another rumor about Missy, this time suggesting she was involved with boys in relationships, including Laura and Karen themselves. They knew this fabricated lie would spark a confrontation between the three friends, counting on Missy's eagerness to mend their bond.

A couple of weeks later, Karen contacted Missy, feigning remorse and proposing a reunion for the three friends. Sadly, in her innocence, Missy agreed to the rendezvous, unknowingly sealing her tragic fate.

The depth of deception was staggering. Even as Missy's family mourned her death, Karen moved into their home, ostensibly to provide support but secretly to manipulate the investigation. She lived among them, sleeping in Missy's bed and sharing meals with her family. Karen's pretense of empathy veiled her true intention: to stay ahead of the investigation and keep their trail cold.

Months stretched on, and Karen's ruse persisted until Eva finally broke her silence. The revelation shattered the family's already fragile peace, exposing the horrific truth that their daughter's killers had been living under their roof. The wheels of justice eventually turned, leading to the conviction of Laura and Karen for Missy's murder. Each received a sentence of 15 years to life in prison. Karen was granted parole in December 2011, while Laura followed suit a year later, in December 2012. The harrowing story of Missy's tragic end served as a reminder of the depths of human cruelty and the darkness that can fester within even the closest of friendships.

"TWISTED FATES: THE TRAGIC DISAPPEARANCE OF RACHEL BARBER"

In 1999, a father went to a train station to pick up his teenage daughter. He waited for the train she was supposed to be on, but when it arrived, he became worried as she didn't get off. Hoping she might be on the next train, he stayed in his parked vehicle at the station.

As time progressed, numerous trains arrived at the station, each one raising his hopes that his daughter would finally emerge. Yet, to his mounting distress, none of these trains carried his missing child. Faced with this bewildering situation, the father eventually departed from the parking lot, holding onto the belief that his daughter had potentially found an alternate means of getting home.

Regrettably, this was far from reality.

Unbeknownst to the father, his daughter had made a pivotal and unfortunate choice on that fateful day. This choice would swiftly propel her entire family into an agonizing and harrowing ordeal, one that would transform their lives into a living nightmare.

In 1998, the Barber family led what could be described as a charmed life. Michael and Elizabeth, together for two decades in a blissful marriage, were parents to three beautiful daughters spanning ages 9 to 15. Residing in an unassuming yet lively home in Melbourne, Australia, the family's humble exterior belied the vibrant atmosphere within. The household resonated with the sounds of children's laughter, intermingled with the joyful conversations of Michael and Elizabeth that echoed through every room.

While the Barbers' existence was far from flawless, overshadowed by financial difficulties that led them to live pay check to pay check, they steadfastly refused to let these challenges define them. Instead, they anchored their identities in a different form of wealth — a wealth of creativity.

Michael, a skilled toy maker and designer, collaborated with Elizabeth, who dedicated herself to the realm of children's literature. The couple's dedication to nurturing creativity was mirrored by their daughters, with each developing their own unique artistic abilities.

At just nine years old, the youngest, Heather, possessed a delightful singing voice that enchanted all who heard it. Middle child Ashley Rose, aged 11, had mastered the flute, displaying her musical prowess. However, it was the oldest daughter, 15-year-old Rachel, who shone brightest in the Barber constellation. Bestowed with the nickname "Rachel Starr," she embodied an exceptional talent for dancing, exuding an air of grace and style so captivating that even her everyday movements appeared as choreographed routines. With striking emerald eyes, fair complexion, and a natural charisma, Rachel's allure effortlessly drew people toward her.

Despite appearances, Rachel confronted her own share of challenges. Excelling academically did not come naturally to her, particularly in subjects like Math and Science that proved overwhelmingly daunting. Moreover, Rachel grappled with an array of acute fears, rendering various aspects of life profoundly difficult. Conversations with strangers were anxiety-inducing, navigating public transportation was a source of dread, and even venturing into stores alone triggered immense unease. Consequently, Rachel relied considerably on her parents, prompting Elizabeth to jestingly label her as "15 going on 12," underscoring her dependence.

In the year 1998, the Barber family's life began to shift as Rachel's anxieties and fears intertwined with her struggles in traditional schoolwork, leading her into a state of depression. Recognizing the need for intervention, her parents embarked on a mission to kindle Rachel's happiness and harness her strengths. It was abundantly clear that Rachel's passion and proficiency lay in dance. Hence, in September of 1998, Michael and Elizabeth resolved to take action. In a bold move, they permitted Rachel to depart from her conventional school path, enrolling her in a full-time dance institution located in Richmond, an inner-city suburb of Melbourne just a 20-minute drive from their family home.

The transformation was remarkable. Once immersed in her new dance school, Rachel flourished. She formed meaningful friendships, delved into modelling, and even found a cherished connection with a boy named Manny. Yet, amid the seemingly positive trajectory of her life, a pivotal choice lay on the horizon, one that would usher in catastrophic consequences.

On a fateful Monday, March 1st of 1999, five months into her enrolment at the new dance school, Rachel, accompanied by her father Michael, embarked on their customary journey from their home to Waddle Park train station. From there, Rachel would board a train bound for Richmond, where she would meet with a friend before making her way to the dance school.

As Michael parked their car at Waddle Park and prepared to bid Rachel farewell, he reminded her of the evening pick-up time, emphasizing that he would return at 6:15 PM. With a smile and an affirmative response, Rachel alighted from the vehicle, met her friend and went about their day.

The day, however, took a sinister turn. As evening descended, Michael awaited Rachel's return at the station. When the train rolled in at 6:15 PM, she was conspicuously absent. Assuming a delay, he anticipated her arrival on the subsequent train. Yet, with each passing train, his anxiety mounted. Darkness descended, further intensifying his apprehension, knowing well Rachel's aversion to being alone in the dark.

Despite his attempts to reassure himself, the truth gradually set in: Rachel was nowhere to be seen. Lacking a cell phone, he was unable to contact her directly. Anxiously, he lingered in the parking lot, witnessing train after train without a sign of his daughter.

Left with no recourse, he eventually departed, driving to his parents' house—a proximity that facilitated communication. Urgently seizing the phone, he dialed his own residence, where Elizabeth, Rachel's mother, answered. His inquiry about Rachel's whereabouts yielded no results. Concern intensified as the realization dawned upon both parents that something was amiss.

Rachel's timeliness and communication habits were crucial

aspects of her personality. Alongside her fear of darkness and unease when alone, these traits made her parents deeply concerned about the situation. Michael promised to come back home quickly, and in his hurry, Elizabeth also took initiative. She called Manny, Rachel's boyfriend, hoping for a glimpse into her daughter's whereabouts.

To her surprise, Manny had last seen Rachel during the day and had not heard from her since. A particular incident at a shopping mall had struck him: Rachel's eagerness to purchase a specific pair of blue chunky platform shoes. This was significant, as Elizabeth recognized the shoes from a recent shopping trip. Unable to afford them, Rachel's intent to buy them seemed puzzling given her financial circumstances.

Further perplexing Elizabeth was Manny's revelation about Rachel's "secret job," a mysterious means by which she intended to afford the extravagant shoes. Rachel had shared scant details with Manny, but her secrecy and the notion of a job involving nighttime activities deeply unsettled Elizabeth.

As the pieces of the puzzle failed to fit, Elizabeth's unease escalated. She began contacting Rachel's friends and haunts, hoping for any hint of her daughter's whereabouts. Regrettably, these efforts yielded no information, propelling the situation further into a crisis.

Amid this escalating worry, Michael returned home and, finding no new leads, decided to head to the police station—a step toward uncovering the truth behind Rachel's sudden disappearance.

Upon reaching the police station, Michael was met with a response that didn't align with his hopes. From the police's perspective, a teenage girl missing for a few hours wasn't deemed an emergency. They assumed that Rachel might have temporarily run off, a scenario that often resolved itself when teenagers returned home in due course. Despite Michael's fervent protestations that his daughter would never voluntarily vanish, the police advised him to wait, assuring him that Rachel would likely reappear.

Despite his inner turmoil, Michael eventually left the station, feeling utterly devastated and fearful for Rachel's well-being. That night, sleep eluded him, as he, his wife, and their other daughters wrestled with the unknown fate of Rachel. With the dawn of a new day, Michael and Elizabeth rushed into the kitchen, hoping that Rachel would have returned. Yet, their anticipations were dashed Rachel remained absent.

As the second day of her disappearance began, a new piece of information emerged. Manny reached out to Michael and Elizabeth, recalling a conversation with Rachel on the day before she vanished. Rachel had reassured Manny about her secret job, asserting its morality and safety due to an old female friend's involvement. This disclosure, while somewhat reassuring given Rachel's fear of solitude, only deepened the mystery surrounding her whereabouts.

The parents contacted Rachel's friends, hoping to uncover more clues. In their inquiries, they discovered that several friends had escorted Rachel to the train station on the day before her disappearance. In fact, some had offered her a ride home, but Rachel had declined, stating that her father would pick her up at Waddle Park at 6:15 PM. The uncertainty of Rachel's intentions—the possibility of either planning to meet her father or intending to embark on the mysterious job—added to the parents' bewilderment.

Michael and Elizabeth's anxiety deepened, leaving them questioning whether they truly understood their daughter. Fears that she might have actually run away began to take root. They found themselves caught in a whirlwind of distress, anxiety, and uncertainty. Struggling to comprehend Rachel's actions, they considered the possibility that they might not have truly known her as well as they believed.

With no clear path forward, the parents resorted to continuing their tireless efforts, scouring everywhere and consulting everyone in their desperate quest to find their missing daughter. Yet, each lead they pursued turned into a dead end, leaving them feeling increasingly hopeless and powerless.

However, on Monday, March 8th, exactly one week after Rachel's disappearance, a glimmer of hope emerged. A girl named Allison, who had attended a dance class with Rachel before she switched schools, learned of Rachel's disappearance through her younger sister. This revelation prompted Allison to take action. She had seen Rachel on the very night she went missing, a full hour after her last confirmed sighting at 6:40 PM.

Alison found herself aboard a train bound for Prahran, a southeastern suburb situated away from Rachel's residence. As the train halted at Richmond station, the doors opened to reveal Rachel and an unfamiliar girl boarding, promptly occupying seats together at the opposite end of the train car. Their camaraderie was unmistakable, as they laughed and engaged in their own world, prompting Alison to politely avert her gaze.

As the journey continued, the trio rode together until their arrival at the Prahran station. Alison prepared to disembark, observing Rachel and the mystery girl rising from their seats, readying to exit the train. In a brief but notable moment, Rachel's eyes met Alison's, leading to a shared smile and wave before the two groups separated. News of this sighting reached Michael and Elizabeth, bringing mixed emotions. On one hand, the revelation hinted at Rachel's company and potentially the fulfilment of her claim to having an older female friend. Yet, the presence of this unknown girl only deepened the mystery. Questions swirled: Were they genuinely friends? Had Rachel and this girl embarked on their secretive pursuit together, only to encounter unforeseen challenges? Or had this girl led Rachel astray, reinforcing the police's initial theory?

With authorities now taking the Barber case more seriously, the focus shifted toward identifying this enigmatic figure. On March 11th, a composite sketch of the mystery girl was crafted based on Alison's description. The police also took measures to trace phone calls made to the Barber residence on the day preceding Rachel's disappearance. The hope was that any communication between Rachel and the mystery girl might provide insight into their activities.

The phone records unveiled a significant lead: a private number had contacted the Barber household twice on the day before Rachel vanished. The first call, lasting 15 minutes, occurred at 5:24 PM, followed shortly by another 30-minute conversation. This discovery prompted further investigation, culminating in the identification of the caller as Caroline Robertson, a 20-year-old woman who strikingly resembled the composite sketch. Caroline's proximity to the Prahran train station, her connection to the Barber family as Rachel's former babysitter, and her resemblance to the mystery girl all aligned to suggest her involvement.

This revelation came as a relief to both the Barbers and the police. The scenario now appeared more plausible: Rachel and Caroline had possibly rendezvoused on the day of Rachel's disappearance, hiding out at Caroline's apartment near the Prahran train station. Buoyed by this discovery and believing they were close to resolving the case, the police set out that evening to Caroline's apartment at 5:25 PM. However, their optimism would soon be met with an unexpected twist.

The police stood before Caroline's front door, knocking and calling out for both Caroline and Rachel. Their calls went unanswered, and the locked door resisted their attempts to gain entry, even with a spare key provided by the property's real estate agent. A specialized latch on the inside seemed to thwart their efforts. Their determination undeterred, the officers explored the building's perimeter in search of alternative access.

As they circled the building, one officer noticed an open second-floor window, wide enough for a person to slip through. The fire department was promptly summoned, and a ladder was placed against the building to reach the window. An officer climbed the ladder and peered into the bedroom beyond the open window. To his shock, he spotted a motionless figure lying face-down at the foot of the bed—it was Caroline. He called for backup, and the apartment was swiftly entered.

Inside, officers discovered Caroline, still alive but unresponsive, and immediately rushed her to the hospital. Meanwhile, the search for Rachel intensified as officers combed through the cluttered and disarrayed apartment. Amidst the disorder, they found no trace of Rachel, except for a bag of clothes that seemed to be her size. The apartment's chaotic appearance suggested that Caroline might have been in the process of moving before her sudden incapacitation.

Within the apartment, officers uncovered items that raised suspicion: rubber gloves, hair dye, bank receipts, and notebooks containing cryptic writings. Hoping to find clues that might lead to Rachel's whereabouts, they collected these items and pressed on in their quest to locate her.

At the hospital, Caroline gradually regained consciousness, although her disorientation persisted. Recognizing the urgency of the situation, medical staff allowed the police to question her immediately. The officers entered her room, and posed the crucial inquiry: "Do you know where Rachel Barber is?"

Caroline's initial response was a stunned silence, followed by a hesitant admission: "Yes." Over the ensuing months, as Caroline's memory gradually reassembled itself, she would recount a story that would astonish Melbourne's police force.

On Sunday, February 28, 1999, the day before Rachel disappeared, Caroline initiated contact. She phoned Rachel with an offer that would ultimately alter both of their destinies. Caroline explained to Rachel that she was conducting a confidential psychology study that required participants. Intrigued, Rachel learned that participating in this study would be financially rewarding. However, due to the confidential nature, Rachel would have to keep it secret. Eager to acquire funds for the coveted blue shoes she desired, Rachel agreed.

The following day, Monday, March 1st, Rachel finished school and met with Caroline at Richmond train station as planned. They boarded a train bound for Prahran, with Allison unwittingly spotting them. Disembarking at Prahran, they progressed to a nearby pizza shop, then walked to Caroline's apartment. Inside, the two of them settled on the bedroom floor, sharing pizza and stories. Subsequently, Caroline initiated the study, beginning with a guided meditation that prompted Rachel to relax and remain calm.

As Rachel complied, Caroline intently watched her, ensuring the drugs she had concealed within the pizza were taking effect. Once she observed Rachel becoming drowsy, Caroline approached and, from behind, looped a telephone cord around␣␣Rachel's neck, tightening it. Rachel, roused from her calm state, fought desperately to remove the cord, but Caroline's weight advantage allowed her to overpower Rachel. As the struggle ensued, Rachel's resistance gradually diminished, and she succumbed.

Caroline loosened the grip, dragged Rachel's lifeless body into a closet, and closed the door. Days later, Caroline pulled Rachel's body from the closet, her life extinguished, and wrapped her in a carpet before stuffing her into a duffel bag. Summoning a taxi, she transported Rachel's body to a rural location near Kilmore, close to her father's vacation home. There, Rachel was buried in a shallow grave beside a childhood pet.

When Caroline was found unconscious in her apartment. It was initially assumed that both she and Rachel might have been attacked, leading to Caroline's unconscious state. However, the actual chain of events was different. Caroline had seen the police arrive at her place, which triggered such immense stress that she suffered a seizure and blacked out in her bedroom.

When Caroline regained consciousness in the hospital, she began explaining that Rachel's death had been accidental. But, as months passed and investigators meticulously examined evidence from Caroline's apartment, a chilling truth emerged. Rachel's demise had not been a mere accident. Among numerous notebooks strewn around Caroline's place, which effectively served as her journals, a disturbing revelation was unveiled.

Within these notebooks, it became evident that Caroline held an intense self-hatred, despising her own physical appearance and her very identity. She fixated on Rachel Barber, a girl she had once babysat – someone she saw as a flawless and beautiful being she yearned to become. This obsession led Caroline to a sinister decision. She resolved to shed her own identity and assume Rachel's by ending her life.

Caroline's plan went far beyond just eliminating Rachel. She aimed to frame the event as Rachel running away, disguising the murder. Following the crime, Caroline had a meticulous transformation strategy laid out. She intended to lose 45 pounds, undergo a nose job to resemble Rachel, and ultimately change her legal name to Rachel Barber. This horrifying plot was slated to culminate in November of 2000, completing Caroline's terrifying transformation.

On Wednesday, March 24, 1999, Rachel Barber's body was laid to rest once more, but this time, she was surrounded by her loved ones, friends, and family. Over 850 people attended her funeral, bringing with them heartfelt letters, poems, and toys, all of which were interred alongside Rachel. Among the items placed with her were the cherished blue shoes that Rachel had desired and planned to purchase with the hundred dollars Caroline had promised her.

In November of 2000, Caroline Robertson admitted guilt in the murder of Rachel Barber and received a 20-year prison sentence. However, in January 2015, Caroline was released after serving just 15 years of that term. In the aftermath of Rachel's tragic passing, her mother, Elizabeth, authored a book titled "The Perfect Victim" recounting the harrowing experience. This book later served as the basis for a major movie, featuring some of Australia's prominent actors and actresses

"UNEARTHLY URGENCY: THE PUZZLING ENCOUNTER THAT SAVED A LIFE ON BULLION BEND"

In the early hours of June 10th, 1994, Deborah Hoyt's world was jolted awake by an inexplicable urgency. She found herself amidst a stay at her relatives' home in Sacramento, California, with plans to remain for a few more days. Yet, something within her compelled her to abandon the comfort of the present and embark on an impromptu journey back to their Lake Tahoe residence.

Awakened by this inner urging, Deborah turned to her husband, eager to share her strange experience. She described the overwhelming need to leave right then and there, an inexplicable force that gnawed at her and refused to be ignored.

Her husband, still groggy from sleep, attempted to rationalize her feelings, suggesting it might be a result of a vivid dream lingering in her waking thoughts. He proposed that she go back to sleep and reassured her that, if the feeling persisted come morning, they could consider leaving.

Reluctantly, Deborah conceded, lying back down to sleep. Yet, the sense of foreboding only grew stronger, an inescapable tug on her instincts. Unable to ignore the sensation any longer, she abruptly rose from bed and declared they needed to leave immediately.

Her husband, slightly exasperated, questioned her urgency, urging her to return to bed and attributing her unease to a mere figment of her imagination. But Deborah's conviction was unyielding. She insisted that they had to depart at once. The urgency was so palpable that her husband finally relented, agreeing to pack their belongings and heed her intuition.

As they gathered their things, Deborah left a note for their relatives, briefly explaining their abrupt departure. Once ready, they set out in their car, leaving their relatives' home behind and venturing into the stillness of the night.

As they navigated through the treacherous Bullion Bend, a winding mountain road known for its hazards, Deborah's intuition would soon be put to the test. Suddenly, the darkness revealed an unsettling sight ahead—a form lying on the side of the road. Initially unclear, the object gradually materialized under the car's headlights, revealing a figure of a woman, unclothed and utterly motionless.

Deborah's heart raced, caught in the eerie grip of fear and determination. She faced her husband, her words rushed and anxious, recounting the unsettling sight of the woman they had just encountered. However as their car carried them closer to the scene, Deborah's fears intensified. A sudden dread settled over her, whispering the chilling possibility that this might be a trap, an orchestrated scenario to lure in unsuspecting Good Samaritans. In the grip of this paranoia, she urged her husband to drive on and find a phone to alert the police.

They arrived at a ranger station, dialed the police, and reported their unsettling encounter. Authorities instructed them to remain in their car while they dispatched officers to investigate. When the officers arrived, they instructed Deborah and her husband to guide them to the location where they had seen the woman.

As the group arrived at the designated spot, Deborah's anxiety only heightened. Her heart raced as the officers scoured the area, their flashlights illuminating the surroundings. After a thorough search, however, their efforts yielded no sign of the woman she had reported. Perplexed, the officers, too, couldn't account for what she had seen.

Amidst this confusion, another officer, Rich Strasser, became intrigued by Deborah's account. Learning that they were searching Bullion Bend, he recalled a recent missing person report involving a woman named Christine Skubish and her young son, Nicky. This report piqued his interest, as their last known whereabouts were consistent with the location Deborah described.

The following morning, Rich woke up early and set out for Bully bend. Once he reached the precise spot Deborah had mentioned, where she claimed to have seen a deceased woman's body, he came across a children's shoe. Stopping his car, he got out and carefully picked up the shoe. He scanned the area, hoping to spot any other unusual items, but the road was devoid of any significant signs. There were no skid marks, debris, or additional clothing.

Rich's curiosity led him to the guardrail that bordered a steep embankment. Peering over the edge, he initially saw a dense spread of trees. However, as he continued to observe, he thought he detected more clothing farther down the slope. This prompted him to take a cautious climb over the guardrail and make his way down.

Within seconds, Rich reached an opening amid the trees and branches, revealing a more level area below. What he encountered was a wrecked red four-door sedan – the same type of car that Christine Skubish had been driving when she went missing. Following the scattered debris, he tracked down the path leading to this mangled vehicle.

Approaching the driver's side, Rich peered inside to find Christine Skubish seated in the driver's seat, unfortunately lifeless. Alongside her was her young son, Nikki, on the passenger seat. Miraculously, Nikki was still alive. He had endured five days without food or water. Medical experts later stated that when Rich discovered him, Nikki likely had a mere one or two hours left before he, too, would have succumbed.

However, a riddle remained, for the timelines didn't align. The fatal car crash that claimed Christine's life had occurred days prior to Deborah's sighting. This incongruence only deepened the mystery surrounding the incident, leaving investigators to grapple with the inexplicable circumstances that led Deborah to witness something seemingly impossible.

The intertwining narratives of Deborah's unshakable intuition, the fleeting apparition of a woman's body, and the discovery of Christine's wreckage created a tapestry of confusion that defied conventional explanations. Deborah's uncanny sense of urgency, matched with the inexplicable timelines, left room for speculation about whether her experience was a mere coincidence or an instance of an otherworldly intervention. One question remained: Did Deborah's intuition and intervention ultimately serve as a guardian angel, guiding Nicky's survival in the face of tragedy?

"DARK DEEDS UNVEILED: THE UNTHINKABLE BETRAYAL OF A FATHER'S TRUST"

In the year 2021, law enforcement officials in Salt Lake City, Utah stumbled upon a perplexing video stored on an individual's phone. Initially appearing somewhat light-hearted, this video takes a disturbing and distressing turn once the true nature of its content becomes apparent.

On January 28, 1976, Daniel Halseth came into the world in the quiet town of Estacada, Oregon, nestled about 30 miles southeast of Portland. Growing up on a family-owned farm, Daniel imbibed a strong work ethic from a young age, arising early to participate in daily chores. This upbringing not only shaped his diligent character but also fostered a deep appreciation for family bonds.

Daniel's high school years marked a period of blossoming for him. Radiating a vibrant smile and a contagious energy, he possessed a natural ability to excel in various pursuits, seemingly effortlessly. Engaging in activities ranging from playing the piano and drums to showcasing remarkable computer and technological skills, Daniel's classmates affectionately dubbed him "drummer Dan." Additionally, his athletic prowess and striking looks made him a charismatic figure that drew people towards him.

However, in 1994, during his junior year of high school, a devastating blow struck Daniel's life. His father, a figure he leaned on for guidance and support, tragically passed away from a brain aneurysm. Despite the immense heartache, Daniel, much like his resilient family, found the strength to persevere.

In 1995, a year after his father's demise, Daniel graduated from high school and pursued higher education in Salem, Oregon. He earned a bachelor's degree in music and later a master's degree in business from a different university in

Salem. It was during this time that he crossed paths with Elizabeth Schworak, a hardworking and accomplished woman who shared his work ethic and talents. Their love story unfolded, culminating in their marriage in 2001.

Their bond thrived, and in due course, they became parents to three children. Establishing their home in Las Vegas, Daniel established a thriving IT company, and their lives were marked by happiness. The couple's journey took a turn when Elizabeth decided to pursue a political career. Running for a state senate seat in Nevada, she embarked on an ambitious campaign that required Daniel to take on the primary role of parenting their children. Despite the challenges, he fully supported her aspirations.

As Elizabeth campaigned, Daniel nurtured their children, provided endless love and care, and managed his growing computer business. His dedication paid off when Elizabeth won the state senate seat on November 2, 2010. Her victory was a testament to the values they both held dear – family, morality, and hard work. At only 27 years old, Elizabeth became the youngest woman ever elected to the

Nevada legislature.

With Elizabeth on the path to political success, it was clear to everyone who knew the Halseth family that Daniel was her most fervent supporter. Their life seemed perfect, a shining example of a close-knit family achieving their dreams. However, their perfect life would soon come crashing down.

Not long after Elizabeth's triumphant election victory, Daniel started noticing her growing closeness with another man named Tiger Helgelien. Tiger, a former golf pro and a rising political star, seemed to be drawing Elizabeth's attention with constant texting and interactions. Frustrated by this, Daniel directly reached out to Tiger, pleading with him to leave his family alone. Despite Daniel's appeals, the communication between Elizabeth and Tiger persisted.

In October 2011, less than a year into Elizabeth's first term as a state senator, Daniel learned that Elizabeth and Tiger had gone on an extended work trip together. This revelation all but confirmed Daniel's suspicions of his wife's affair. Confronting Elizabeth about her infidelity, their argument escalated, with Daniel expressing his anger and frustration verbally but not physically. Elizabeth eventually told him to stop, and he complied.

Over the following days, the couple attended therapy sessions in an attempt to salvage their marriage. However, their marriage was hanging by a thread. On October 21st, Elizabeth contacted the police, accusing Daniel of inappropriate touching during their argument about the affair. Shockingly, Daniel was arrested and charged with "open and gross lewdness," a charge that often involves unwanted touching. This accusation is known to be prone to false claims, as no physical proof is required for arrest.

After being found guilty of the charge, Daniel faced six months of probation, anger management, and the stigma of being a registered sex offender. The already strained marriage between Elizabeth and Daniel spiraled into a bitter and highly publicized divorce. Elizabeth, who had built her political campaign on family values, faced a barrage of rumors about her affair and her husband's conviction. She resigned from her state senate seat in February 2012, and their divorce was finalized later that year.

Despite having been the primary parent for years, Daniel's status as a registered sex offender led to him being denied custody of their children. Elizabeth gained custody and left for Alaska with her three kids, ultimately marrying Tiger Helgelien. For Daniel, this was an immense blow, as he cherished his role as a father. Though heartbroken, he found solace in his computer business and made every effort to stay connected to his children.

In the midst of his struggles, Daniel met Bogdana, whom he married. He seemingly found a new direction in life and maintained a positive social media presence. However, his second marriage also ended in divorce in 2019, leaving him feeling alone once more.

Just when it seemed like life might crumble for Daniel, an incredible turn of events brought a glimmer of hope. His first ex-wife, Elizabeth, and their three kids decided to leave Alaska and resettle in Las Vegas, Nevada. This wasn't an attempt to reconcile; Elizabeth simply liked living in Las Vegas and wanted to return. Daniel, overjoyed by the prospect of seeing his kids regularly, embraced this opportunity. By late 2020, his youngest daughter, Sierra, had essentially moved back in with him, even though legally she wasn't supposed to.

In August of that year, while Sierra was living with him, Daniel decided to take Elizabeth to court to gain custody of Sierra, who was just 16 years old at the time. In court sessions recorded on video, Daniel passionately argued that Elizabeth's home was toxic, especially for Sierra, who was struggling with mental health issues. He emphasized the therapy he had enrolled her in and even presented a letter from Sierra supporting the idea of living with him.

Elizabeth countered by calling Daniel a liar, suggesting that he wasn't fit to be a parent and casting doubt on the authenticity of the letter. The judge, growing increasingly frustrated with the ongoing feud, admonished both parents for creating a harmful environment for their children.

After months of legal battles and negotiations, the judge ordered Sierra to return to her mother's residence in early 2021, adhering to legal custody arrangements. However, Sierra's connection with her father was strong, and she eventually sneaked out of her mother's house to be with him.

The custody dispute continued, with Sierra still choosing to stay with her father despite court orders and her mother's pleas. In April 2021, an unusual incident occurred: money was withdrawn from Daniel's shared bank account with his second ex-wife, Bogdana. These unauthorized withdrawals raised suspicion and were flagged as potentially fraudulent, leading to notifications being sent to both Daniel and Bogdana.

Bogdana, aware that these withdrawals were not her doing, attempted to contact Daniel, but he didn't respond. Concerned about his unusual silence, she reached out to Daniel's mother, Christine, who contacted Sierra to inquire about Daniel's well-being. Sierra's response indicated that his phone was acting up but that he would be fine by the next night.

However, as the hours passed, neither Christine nor Bogdana heard from Daniel, and their concern grew. Christine reached out to Sierra again, and this time, the responses were becoming increasingly evasive. With her instincts alert, Christine knew something was wrong, especially when

Sierra didn't answer her phone calls and sent messages that seemed out of character.

Despite the oddity of the situation, Christine initially tried to let it go, assuming she would hear from Daniel soon. But by the next day, when Daniel remained unresponsive, Christine's worry escalated. She reached out to Sierra again, demanding to speak to Daniel. Sierra's response, claiming Daniel was in the shower and couldn't talk, didn't ease Christine's apprehensions. Her motherly intuition told her that something was amiss, and she knew action was needed to ensure Daniel and Sierra were okay.

Christine's concern led her to reach out to Peggy Newman, who was both Daniel's landlord and a close friend. Christine asked Peggy if she could perform a welfare check at Daniel's house. Peggy, understanding the urgency, agreed to help but mentioned it would take a few hours before she could get there.

Though she knew Peggy was on her way, Christine's anxiety grew, and at 1:46 p.m., unable to wait any longer, she called the police herself to request a welfare check. In the 911 call, she expressed her worry and the circumstances leading up to her concern, explaining that Daniel had been missing for two days despite numerous attempts to reach him.

Just a few minutes after Christine's 911 call, Peggy Newman and a friend of hers arrived at Daniel's residence even before the police. Approaching the front door, they noticed that Daniel's blue Nissan Altima was absent from the driveway. Knocking on the door and receiving no response, they tried the doorknob and found it unlocked. Gaining access to the house, they entered.

Shortly thereafter, Peggy and her friend emerged from the house, visibly distressed. Peggy immediately called 911 to report what she had encountered to the dispatcher. She described her discovery with urgency and anxiety, conveying the unsettling scene they had encountered inside the house.

When the police finally arrived at Daniel's residence on April 9th, they encountered Peggy Newman and her friend, both appearing distressed and anxious on the sidewalk. After speaking with them, the officers entered the house and were confronted with the same disturbing scene that had shocked Peggy and her friend earlier. However, the police were confounded by the puzzling nature of the situation; the pieces didn't seem to fit together logically.

A day earlier, surveillance cameras captured a man and a woman using Daniel's debit card to withdraw cash from various Las Vegas ATMs. The same couple was later recorded on camera entering a local supermarket called WinCo, where they used Daniel's debit card to purchase a few items. After leaving the supermarket, they proceeded to a Las Vegas Home Depot, where they once again used Daniel's debit card for a small purchase.

Following these activities, the man and woman arrived at Daniel's residence, where they spent the night.

After four days, on April 13th, law enforcement in Salt Lake City, Utah, coincidentally stumbled upon the man and woman who had been caught on camera using Daniel's debit card at WinCo and Home Depot on April 8th. The police encountered them while they were on a bus in Salt Lake City. A search of their belongings, including their phones, yielded a video that the couple had recorded over the preceding days. This footage contained crucial information about the interior of Daniel's house. The transcript of the video showcases 18-year-old Aaron Guerrero and his 16-year-old girlfriend Sierra Halseth, both appearing cheerful and laughing:

Aaron: "Welcome back to our YouTube channel." Sierra: "Day 3..." Aaron: "Day 3 after taking someone's life." Sierra: "Whoa, don't capture that on camera." Aaron "it was worth it".

On the fateful morning of April 8th, Sierra Halseth, a 16-year-old, allegedly, in a disturbing turn of events, collaborated with her boyfriend, Aaron Guerrero. Their actions would soon thrust them into the center of a chilling and horrifying narrative that defied comprehension.

Their day commenced with a calculated purpose, as Aaron and Sierra embarked on a series of seemingly mundane yet deeply unsettling tasks. They withdrew substantial amounts of money from various ATMs scattered across the city, thereby securing the resources they deemed necessary for their ominous plans.

Their journey took them to a nearby store, a WinCo supermarket, where they gathered an unsettling assortment of items: disposable gloves, bleach, and drop cloths. These seemingly innocuous purchases concealed a far more sinister purpose that was gradually coming to light. Their disturbing shopping spree carried on at a Home Depot, where they procured even more ominous tools: a circular saw, saw blades, and lighter fluid.

Armed with these chilling supplies, Sierra and Aaron's next destination was Daniel's house—the very place that once stood as a bastion of familial love and warmth.

Within those walls, an unthinkable betrayal unfolded. Sierra, Daniel's own daughter, and her boyfriend Aaron seemed to carry out actions that defied understanding and shook the very foundations of trust within a family. While the exact details of what transpired within the confines of that home are veiled in secrecy, it's possible to draw haunting inferences from the available information.

What allegedly occurred next was a sequence of unspeakable violence. Sierra and Aaron purportedly subjected Daniel to a barrage of horrifying stab wounds—up to 70, concentrated primarily at the back of his head. The motivations that drove this brutality remain elusive, and the manner in which they extinguished Daniel's life challenges our capacity to comprehend the incomprehensible.

Following this horrific act, Sierra and Aaron allegedly placed Daniel's lifeless body inside a sleeping bag. They then desecrated his remains further by dousing him with lighter fluid, before igniting a fire that turned a space of shared memories into a grim tableau of horror. In that very living room, where laughter and togetherness once thrived, they committed an act of unthinkable callousness.

As the flames subsided and the echoes of their malevolence lingered, Sierra and Aaron's actions took an even darker turn. Attempting to dismember Daniel's body with the tools they had obtained, they encountered obstacles that prevented them from fully carrying out their sinister plan. In a futile attempt to cleanse the crime scene of evidence, they resorted to bleach, which proved ineffective in erasing the traces of their heinous actions.

In a final act of desperation, they sought to incinerate the entire house—a bid to erase any lingering evidence of their deeds. However, their attempt fell short, leaving behind a grim testament to the horrors that had occurred within those walls.

The aftermath of their terrifying spree led Sierra and Aaron on a path of escape that culminated in their apprehension in Salt Lake City. The discovery of Aaron's unpaid bus fare caught the attention of authorities and inadvertently exposed their chilling plot.

Now, as Sierra and Aaron await trial, the intricate web of motivations, the depths of their alleged involvement, and the disturbing psychology behind their actions remain the subject of intense scrutiny.

"A TALE OF TWO LIVES: THE TRAGIC COLLISION OF WHITNEY CERAK AND LAURA VAN RYN"

On the morning of Wednesday, April 26, 2006, the vibrant and sociable 18-year-old Whitney Cerak embarked on her journey across her college campus, destined for a lecture hall where she had a class scheduled. As a freshman at Taylor University—a renowned Evangelical Christian liberal arts college nestled in Upland, Indiana—Whitney's path intersected with fellow students bustling toward their respective classes. Amid the commotion, an unexpected pang of anxiety surged within her. The approach of the school year's end triggered mixed emotions in Whitney. While the prospect of returning to her rural hometown of Gaylord, Michigan for summer vacation was exciting, the thought of parting from the friends she had made in college weighed heavily on her heart.

Upland, a small town situated between the larger cities of Indianapolis and Fort Wayne, was home to Taylor University. Whitney had crafted a close-knit circle of friends during her freshman year, primarily among fellow newcomers. However, her curiosity and desire to learn from those with more experience led her to foster connections with upperclassmen. She had quickly discovered that their guidance and expertise were valuable assets, willingly shared by those who had walked the collegiate path before her.

As she navigated the campus, Whitney chanced upon a sign soliciting student volunteers for an upcoming banquet in honor of the university's new president. Intrigued, she inquired and learned that most of the volunteers were upperclassmen. Without hesitation, Whitney added her name to the list, recognizing the potential for both service and interaction with those who had a wealth of experience to offer.

The remainder of that day flowed in its accustomed rhythm for Whitney—attending classes, connecting with friends, and finally retreating to her dorm room as the evening approached. Unbeknownst to her, the mundane pattern of her day was a prelude to an impending tragedy that would soon shatter her world.

Awakening the following morning, Whitney adhered to her routine—showering, brushing her teeth, and meticulously selecting an outfit for the day ahead. While not overly concerned with her appearance, she understood that the day would be spent among upperclassmen and university staff, prompting her to present herself in the best light possible. Casting a final glance in her mirror, she felt a fleeting sense of pride. The reflection staring back at her embodied the achievements and growth she had experienced during her freshman year—a year marked by academic success, personal development, and the forging of new friendships.

As the clock ticked and time pressed on, Whitney departed her room, bound for the day's activities. Along the way, she encountered a group of fellow students huddled near a university van. Drawn to their presence, she introduced herself to the group of seven other Taylor students, most of whom were seniors, accompanied by a university staff member. A sense of camaraderie permeated their interactions, and soon after her arrival, the group was ushered onto the van, embarking on a journey north toward Fort Wayne.

As the van hummed along the highway, Whitney struck up a conversation with Laura Van Wren, a 22-year-old senior who exuded an aura of warmth and friendliness. Despite their initial unfamiliarity, Whitney quickly discovered a surprising amount of common ground with Laura. Their shared physical attributes—both tall, blonde, and slender—prompted inquiries from their fellow volunteers regarding their potential relation. Beyond their physical similarities, Laura hailed from Caledonia, a small rural Michigan town located a mere couple of hours south of Gaylord, Whitney's hometown.

Upon reaching their destination—an hour's drive from the campus—Whitney and her fellow volunteers poured their efforts into setting up the banquet hall for the next day's ceremony. As they arranged tables, placed silverware, and adorned the venue with decorations, Whitney and Laura maintained a close bond, engaging in light-hearted conversation as they worked. Throughout the day, their camaraderie blossomed, a testament to the connection they had forged in such a short span of time.

By 7 PM, with the banquet hall perfectly prepared for the upcoming event, the group concluded their efforts and exited the venue. Reuniting with the van, they embarked on their journey back to campus.

During the initial minutes of the ride, Laura and Whitney engaged in continuous conversation, their voices weaving a tapestry of connection and camaraderie. However, as the journey progressed, the other members of the volunteer group succumbed to the exhaustion of their day's efforts. Gradually, conversations dwindled, replaced by a tranquil silence. Gazing out of the van's windows, each person retreated into their own thoughts, absorbed in the passing scener

Approximately half an hour later, as the van drew closer to the university campus, Whitney's gaze shifted momentarily from the window to Laura beside her. In that fleeting moment, their eyes locked—a fleeting connection that conveyed volumes without a word spoken. Whitney offered a slightly awkward smile, met with a reciprocating smile from Laura. Yet, within the confines of that moment, an oddity caught Whitney's attention. There was a bright light on the side of Laura's face, in the span of mere seconds, the intensity of that light escalated dramatically. A blinding radiance engulfed the van's interior, transforming the mundane setting into a surreal scene. Abruptly, a voice erupted from the front of the van—a startled exclamation of "Oh my God." The once-bustling atmosphere yielded to an eerie stillness, enveloping the van in an unsettling hush.

Within a matter of minutes, the chaotic aftermath of the accident unfurled. A torrent of urgent 9-1-1 calls inundated dispatch centers from alarmed motorists traversing I-69. First Responders, anticipating a grim scene, hastened to the site with a somber resolve. However, even their seasoned expectations fell short of what they encountered. The northbound and southbound lanes of I-69 near Taylor University bore witness to a devastating spectacle. Debris, shards of jagged metal, and fragments of shattered glass were strewn across the road. Amid this wreckage lay the harrowing evidence of a tragic collision—the lives of the van's occupants irrevocably altered.

The source of the blinding light that Whitney had glimpsed, was unveiled as a massive, fully loaded tractor-trailer truck weighing a staggering 80,000 pounds. Behind the wheel was Robert Spencer, a truck driver who had succumbed to drowsiness, allowing his vehicle to drift from its course. Careening off the road into the grassy median, the truck careened into the southbound lane, colliding violently with the van carrying Laura and Whitney.

The collision's impact was cataclysmic, stripping away a significant portion of the van's side and initiating a frenzied spin. Inside the van, occupants were flung with brutal force into the tumult of the roadway. In the aftermath, First Responders grappled with the grim sight before them. Robert remained within his truck, miraculously alive. However, within the van's wreckage, the terrible truth emerged—five of the nine occupants had succumbed to the impact.

As dawn broke on April 27th, in the serene Michigan town of Gaylord, Whitney Sarek's family received a chilling phone call. The Grant County coroner's somber voice shattered the tranquility, delivering the heart-wrenching news of their daughter's untimely demise. The stark contrast of life and death was underscored as, hours later and miles apart, the Van Ryn family in Caledonia, Michigan received their own call—Laura had survived the ordeal, albeit in a critical state.

In the days that ensued, the Sarek family commenced the painful process of arranging Whitney's funeral, an event constrained by the extent of her injuries, requiring a closed casket. Meanwhile, the Van Ryn family's attention shifted towards aiding Laura's delicate recuperation. Laura was transported to a rehabilitation center in Grand Rapids, Michigan, which specialized in treating brain injuries. The course of Laura's future remained shrouded in uncertainty.

As the Cerick family bid their final farewell to Whitney during a visitation on April 29th—three days post-accident—over 1,400 individuals from Gaylord and beyond attended, a poignant testament to the deep impact she had made on their lives.

The day following Whitney's poignant visitation, on April 30th, her remains were laid to rest. Simultaneously, in an unexpected twist, Laura's family, who had vigilantly maintained a continuous bedside presence in Grand Rapids, received an astonishing update. Grounded in promising brain scans, there emerged a glimmer of hope—Laura's impending emergence from her coma seemed increasingly likely. However, despite these encouraging signs, no precise timeline could be discerned. Over the ensuing weeks, Laura remained ensconced in a comatose state, though her body embarked on a slow but steady journey towards recovery. As the days advanced, whispers of a potential revival materialized.

On the 16th of May, twenty days after the heart-wrenching accident, a remarkable awakening transpired—Laura, against the odds, emerged from her coma. Initial signs were promising; her cognitive faculties appeared intact. A sense of miraculous triumph enveloped the Van Ryn family as Laura's steady recuperation journey commenced. Progress was evidenced by her gradual regaining of physical strength, enabling her to manipulate her limbs and even sit upright in her hospital bed. However, beneath this veneer of improvement, a disconcerting revelation loomed.

A pivotal moment unfolded on May 22nd, a week after Laura's reawakening. A physical therapist, accompanied by her family, handed Laura a pencil and paper, urging her to write down a specific word—one familiar to her, one that she ought to be able to spell. As she laboriously etched the chosen word, an alarming revelation dawned—the word she inscribed was incorrect. This unsettling turn of events raised concerns about the extent of her brain injury. Yet, the truth that would eventually surface would dwarf any previous assumptions.

In the wake of the accident on April 26th, the immediate response was characterized by swift and organized chaos. First Responders moved purposefully among the wreckage, striving to distinguish the living from the deceased. When they discovered Laura at the scene, her life hung in the balance. Swiftly, she was carefully placed onto a stretcher. Her purse, containing her driver's license, was bundled alongside her, and together they were loaded into an awaiting ambulance headed for the hospital. Within the hospital's confines, Laura's identity was established using her driver's license, an essential piece of information for medical records and identification purposes. Her injuries necessitated comprehensive attention, this meticulous process involved the careful placement of bandages and casts, crafting an intricate mosaic that mirrored the contours of her body.

In the weeks that ensued, the gradual unveiling of Laura's injuries underscored the profound transformation her body had undergone. One distinct alteration, her dental structure, was glaringly apparent; her teeth bore a distinct shift, an indelible mark of the trauma she had endured. However, to her family, her altered appearance paled in comparison to the miracle of her continued existence. Their focus was resolute—Laura was alive, and that was all that truly mattered.

Amidst these unfolding events, the fateful day of May 22nd was marred by a revelation that struck with the force of a thunderbolt. On Monday, May 22nd, when Laura was given a piece of paper and a pencil and asked to write her name, a fateful error unfolded. Instead of writing "L-A-U-R-A" for Laura, she inscribed "W-H-I-T-N-E-Y." This seemingly small action would later reveal a massive blunder that had gone unnoticed until that very moment. The woman sitting in the hospital bed, clutching the pencil and paper, was not the 22-year-old Laura Van Wren; rather, she was the 18-year-old Whitney Cerak. A gut-wrenching reality emerged—a misinterpretation had triggered a sequence of events leading to an agonizing case of mis identity.

Upon discovering Whitney on the

roadside, clinging to life, the First Responders initially assumed that the purse beside her belonged to her. In light of this, they decided to open the wallet they found nearby, which contained a driver's license. Astonishingly, the appearance of the person on the ground bore such an uncanny resemblance to the photo on the license that they erroneously concluded it was Laura. Adding to the twist of fate, Whitney's purse, complete with her driver's license, had fortuitously landed close to Laura's body. This unfortunate series of events culminated in the tragic misidentification of Laura as Whitney Cerak.

The profound implications of this revelation were seismic. Whitney's grieving family, previously resigned to the loss of their beloved daughter, were now confronted with a living miracle. The news that Whitney was alive—a stark contrast to the reality they had accepted—defied comprehension. A plane journey to Grand Rapids and a tearful reunion with their daughter affirmed the unthinkable—Whitney was alive, embracing them with outstretched arms.

Undoubtedly a miraculous turn of events for the Cerak family, this revelation simultaneously unfurled as a heart-wrenching nightmare for the Van Ryn's upon discovering the mistaken identity. Lingering suspicions had already infiltrated their thoughts concerning their daughter, most notably her teeth, which appeared distinctively different from their recollections. Despite these reservations, medical professionals and others had provided reassurances that significant accidents could bring about notable alterations in both appearance and behavior. Consequently, the Van Ryn's chose to set aside their apprehensions, focusing instead on tending to their child's well-being and supporting her recovery.

Several days later, Laura Van Ryn's remains, which had been interred under the tombstone bearing the name Whitney Cerak in Gaylord, Michigan, were exhumed. Her body was then transported to Caledonia, where the Van Ren family was finally able to provide their daughter with a befitting funeral and a dignified burial.

Although Whitney and Laura had only briefly crossed paths during the volunteer event in Fort Wayne, their families found solace in their shared ordeal. In 2008, precisely two years after the harrowing crash, the Cerak's and the Van Ryn's united to co-author a book chronicling their experiences from each family's perspective. This book, titled "Mistaken Identity: Two Families, One Survivor, Unwavering Hope," delved into the depths of their intertwined journeys through this nightmarish event.

In the same year, on April 26th, marking the second anniversary of the tragic accident, Taylor University commemorated the lives of the five victims by dedicating a prayer chapel in their honor. In the aftermath of the crash, Indiana overhauled its protocols and procedures for identifying accident victims, implementing stringent measures to prevent any recurrence of such a grievous mix-up.

As for Robert Spencer, the truck driver responsible for the catastrophic accident, he faced the consequences of his actions. He was sentenced to a four-year prison term.

"TWISTED TRUTHS AND TRAGIC CONSEQUENCES: THE UNBELIEVABLE SAGA OF RYAN WALLER'S INTERROGATION"

In 2006, Heather Quan was a 21-year-old college student living in the small residential town of Desert Hills in Arizona. From a very young age, Heather was someone who always seemed to give her friendship to the people who needed it the most—people who were hurting on the inside or whose society had kind of forgotten about her. This is why, as a teenager and a young adult, she would often spend her weekends volunteering her time with underprivileged children. It's also why she aspired to go to law school and become a defense lawyer because she loved the idea of professionally helping people that desperately needed her assistance.

She lived in a rental home with her 18-year-old boyfriend named Ryan Waller. Among other things, he was an enthusiastic gun collector and a student at the time. The couple had plans to visit Ryan's father, Don, on Christmas Day—specifically on December 25th. However, when the day arrived and Don had prepared dinner for them, expecting their visit, they didn't show up. Don attempted to contact both of them, but when he couldn't reach either, a sense of unease settled in. Their failure to appear was highly uncharacteristic. Instead of driving over to their property himself, Don contacted the local police and requested a welfare check.

The police arrived at the house in Desert Hills, Arizona. They knocked on the door, but there was no answer. They looked in the windows, and some lights were on, but it was mostly dark inside. They couldn't really tell from the car in the driveway if it belonged to the homeowners or somebody else. So, they stood there for a second, looking in the windows. There was no movement. They knocked again while simultaneously calling out, 'Hey, we're the police. We're here to do a welfare check, just want to make sure you guys are okay.'

This time, after they were done knocking, they heard the deadbolt unlock, and then the door swung inward into the house. Standing right in front of them was Ryan. Ryan had this huge bruise on his left eye, this big black eye, and he had a cut on his nose. He was just standing there, not saying anything, not asking any questions, just looking at them. They looked past Ryan into his house, and they saw a woman lying on the couch, which they presumed was his girlfriend Heather, the two people they were coming to look for.

So, they turned their attention back to Ryan and asked him, 'You know what happened to your eye?' Ryan was a little bit cagey; he didn't really give them a straight answer. He basically said, 'You know, I don't know. I don't know what happened to my eye.' The police didn't really pry that much, but eventually, they determined that Ryan was more or less okay, albeit a little bit strange. They said, 'Okay, well, who's the woman lying on the couch? Is that Heather?' Ryan again was kind of cagey and a little bit dismissive. He said something along the lines of, 'Oh, you know, she's just sleeping.'

The police said to him, 'Look, we're here on a welfare check. Your father sent us here to check on you guys. We have to go in there and wake her up, make sure she's okay.' Ryan was a bit weird, kind of defensive, and didn't immediately comply, but eventually stepped out of the way. The police walked into the residence, walked over to the couch. As soon as they looked down at the girl on the couch, they saw right away that she was not asleep; she was dead. She had been for at least a couple of days. She had died from a single gunshot wound to the head.

Immediately, Ryan was arrested and brought out to a squad car. He didn't fight the arrest, but he emphatically said he didn't know what was going on, didn't understand what was happening. He didn't know what happened to Heather; he just seemed generally confused. Regardless, he was thrown in the back of the police car outside the property, and he would sit there for several hours while more and more police and paramedics arrived to process the crime scene and transfer Heather's body to a morgue."

Finally, around 5 am on December 26th, the police brought Ryan, who after all these hours was still in the back of the police car, to the Phoenix police station for questioning. The ensuing interrogation, which spanned an hour and was fully recorded, began somewhat conventionally. However, it swiftly spiraled into an utterly peculiar and unpredictable exchange between Ryan and the detective leading the questioning. As the interrogation reached its conclusion, an astonishing revelation would come to light. Once you uncover the truth of what transpired, your truly will be shocked to the core.

In the video, Ryan is led into a nondescript, small interrogation room at 5:08 am on December 26th. Having just arrived at the station, he is placed in this room. He is dressed in a white jumpsuit, which might have been issued by the police or possibly owned by him, although it certainly resembles prison attire more closely. He is without shoes and socks, and his hands are not cuffed. He proceeds to enter the room, taking a seat in the back corner of the interrogation room. This chair is positioned adjacent to a table, with another chair on the opposite side. Ryan settles into the corner chair, oriented somewhat towards the center of the room. He remains quiet, exhibiting minimal movement. At some juncture, he becomes aware of a handcuff affixed to the table. While there are instances where the police would secure the person being interviewed with handcuffs, Ryan is not instructed to use the handcuff in this case. As a result, he remains uncuffed, with no directive to attach the handcuff… however Ryan handcuffs himself to the table anyway, turns and places his arms over it, resting his head on his arms. He remains in this position for about five minutes, emitting occasional groaning sounds, yet predominantly maintaining silence. Unexpectedly, as he lies there, he emits a rather loud moan and abruptly rises from his chair, as if intending to exit the room. However, the unanticipated obstacle of the handcuff prevents his departure, the very handcuff he hadn't been instructed to fasten. Despite this restraint, he doesn't display much perturbation, appearing somewhat perplexed by the situation. Yet, his

bewilderment is fleeting; he extends his arm across the table and seizes a blank sheet of paper before reseating himself. Crossing his legs, he becomes absorbed in scrutinizing the paper, marking the time as 5:17 a.m. –

approximately nine minutes into this still-uninitiated interrogation.

At this point, as Ryan engrosses himself in the blank paper, Detective Dalton enters the interrogation room. Dalton informs Ryan of their intent to photograph his feet, instructing him to place his feet onto the adjacent table. Initially, Ryan's response reflects his confusion, struggling to grasp the purpose behind this directive. Nevertheless, he eventually acquiesces, positioning his feet on the table. During this process, another officer enters the room, carrying a camera and an extensive kit. Over the next ten minutes, this officer undertakes the task of photographing and swabbing Ryan's feet. Throughout this ten-minute interval, Dalton remains present, and Ryan intermittently inquires about the possibility of departing and returning home. These queries betray his apparent lack of awareness regarding the gravity of his situation. When met with Dalton's negative response, Ryan's demeanor shifts into one of palpable frustration, conveying a mixture of anger and disappointment akin to a child.

At 5:28 a.m., following the completion of this ten-minute session during which Ryan's feet were photographed and swabbed, the second officer exits the room. Dalton closes the door behind him before proceeding to pull a chair from the opposite side of the table, situating it closer to Ryan. Taking a seat, Dalton introduces himself and initiates the conversation by posing some fundamental questions. He requests confirmation of Ryan's name, to which Ryan complies, and subsequently inquires about his date of birth and social security number, receiving affirmative responses from Ryan for both queries.

Dalton then proceeds to ask Ryan if he comprehends the reason for his presence in the interrogation room, and Ryan responds negatively. In response, Dalton suggests suspending their current line of inquiry and expresses his intention to read Ryan his Miranda rights. This particular juncture marks the onset of Ryan's increasingly peculiar behavior during the interrogation.

Upon hearing Dalton's intent to read his rights, Ryan appears to struggle in processing the information, wearing a blank expression. Sensing Ryan's confusion, Dalton lightens the mood by referencing the portrayal of such scenarios on television shows like "Cops," "Law & Order," and "CSI," where characters are read their rights. In response, Ryan simply utters a monosyllabic "no." Dalton, taken aback, queries whether Ryan has never watched any crime show where rights are read, to which Ryan's demeanor shifts from robotic compliance to a more defensive posture. He claims to have seen such shows, albeit unconvincingly. This minor falsehood raises a peculiar tension, as both individuals share a moment of silence, characterized by Dalton's awareness of Ryan's untruth and Ryan's apparent confusion. Ultimately, Dalton chooses not to focus on this insignificant lie and proceeds to read Ryan his rights before returning to the line of questioning.

At this point, Dalton resumes his inquiry with more basic questions.

In the subsequent part, Ryan's behavior continues to be observed.

When Dalton inquires about the highest grade Ryan achieved in school, Ryan avoids eye contact with Dalton and instead looks towards the far side of the room. Ryan responds with a perplexed "I don't know," prompting Dalton to inquire if he doesn't know the grade level he attained. Ryan replies with "No, I don't know, uh, eighth, eighth grade." This swift alteration in response under challenge leads Dalton to suspect that Ryan might be lying, although the matter is relatively trivial. However, despite the insignificance, this pattern of mistrust accumulates, making it challenging for Dalton to have faith in Ryan's honesty, particularly when he struggles to provide accurate responses even to unimportant inquiries.

Nevertheless, Dalton chooses not to dwell on this minor inconsistency, opting to continue his questioning. He then proceeds to ask a follow-up question, based on Ryan's claim that he completed eighth grade. Dalton inquires whether Ryan obtained his General Educational Development (GED) certificate, which is equivalent to a high school diploma and is typically pursued by individuals who didn't graduate high school. While the answer should be a binary choice – either having a GED or not – Ryan's response is anything but clear-cut. His contradictory and puzzling response highlights a facet of Ryan that doesn't align with expectations, leading to confusion. Ryan's response to Dalton's query about the GED includes phrases like "I don't know, I don't know, I don't know, I don't know" and "I just want to go home".

Dalton then attempts to clarify Ryan's educational background by asking about the highest grade he completed. Ryan initially responds with a simple "no," misunderstanding Dalton's question as referring to letter grades. Dalton rephrases the question to directly ask if Ryan graduated high school. Ryan's straightforward "no" implies that he didn't graduate high school, and the highest level he completed was eighth grade.

The dialogue shifts as Dalton inquires if Ryan possesses reading and writing skills, to which Ryan straightforwardly responds with a simple "yeah."

As the discussion about Ryan's education reaches an impasse, Dalton decides not to dwell on the issues with

Ryan's answers thus far. Instead, he continues to ask more questions, including addressing Heather, Ryan's girlfriend. Dalton, aware that Heather is deceased, queries whether Ryan has a girlfriend. Despite knowing the truth, Dalton aims to have Ryan affirm his relationship with Heather. Ryan denies having a girlfriend, a falsehood, and Dalton proceeds by asking if Ryan knows a girl named Heather. Ryan acknowledges knowing Heather, yet his description of her is incorrect. He mentions that Heather was a 16 or 17-year-old girl, despite her actual age being 21. Additionally, Ryan inaccurately provides a last name of "Kaiman" instead of Heather's real last name, "Quan." Dalton recognizes these discrepancies but does not overly focus on them, choosing instead to continue his line of questioning.

Dalton then inquires about a bruise on Ryan's face, which Ryan initially claims not to know the cause of. When Dalton persists and probes further about the bruise, Ryan begins to open up about it.

The interrogation continues between Ryan and Dalton:
Dalton: "What happened to your

face?" Ryan: "I don't know." Dalton: "You told the officer just a few minutes ago that someone hit you. Do you remember who hit you?" Ryan: "Oh, I don't know. I think it was Heather." Dalton: "Why would Heather hit you?" Ryan: "I don't know. That's an accident. I forgot why."

Like the other police officers involved, Dalton believed going into this interrogation that Ryan killed Heather. The bruise on his face was assumed to be a result of Heather fighting back before Ryan ultimately killed her. So, for Ryan to attribute the mark on his face to Heather, even though he claimed it was an accident, was tantamount to admitting to the killing. Dalton sought to extract more specific details about the actual physical struggle that occurred between Ryan and Heather. However, as he continued asking questions with increasing intensity, Ryan became more defensive and started providing seemingly random pieces of information. Much of what he said appeared untrue; for instance, he suggested that there were two or three other people in the house on the night Heather was killed. It appears Ryan was panicking and uttering a stream of disparate statements.

Recognizing the conversation was spiraling out of control, Dalton attempted to regain focus. He interrupted Ryan, expressing that the situation was becoming chaotic, and said, "Ryan, there is a dead girl in your house, and I need information."

Ryan: "Huh... huh." Dalton: "There's a dead girl in your living room." Ryan: "She's dead." Dalton: "Yes." Ryan: "Heather." Dalton: "I don't know. I want to know what happened in your house last night." Ryan: "The girl on the couch is dead." Dalton: "I don't know... if she's on the couch... she's dead."

The interesting thing about Ryan's reaction to being told by Dalton for the first time in the interrogation that there was a dead girl in his house is that Ryan reacted with genuine surprise. It's the only time in the entire interrogation, from start to finish, where Ryan sits forward in his chair, kind of perking up, and he seems relatively normal. He's not acting confused and bizarre. It's as if he hadn't heard this information before, that he didn't know Heather was dead, and he's now, for the first time, being told. It shocked his system. However, just seconds after he sits forward and seems engaged, he reverts back to his bizarre behavior. He suddenly crafts an elaborate story about what happened to Heather, even though just seconds ago it seemed like he had just learned about it. This quick shift doesn't make much sense – having a story so readily available for something he seemed to know nothing about. And of course, like all his other answers, the story he gave was full of contradictions, holes, and was simply unbelievable.

Ryan: "Well, these people came over – Ritchie and his dad – with shooting arrow bow and darts, you know what I'm talking about?" Dalton: "Yeah." Ryan: "They hit me and her with those, that's it." Dalton: "They hit you... and they hit you?" Ryan: "Yeah." Dalton: "Now it's Ritchie that hit you, not Heather?" Ryan: "No, Ritchie and his dad, Ritchie's dad." Dalton: "They hit you?" Ryan: "Yes." Dalton: "Why?" Ryan: "Because they're trying to get their stuff, I don't know why." Dalton: "And they had some kind of bow and arrows?" Ryan: "They each had two revolvers and they didn't let off any shells." Dalton: "Okay, you just said they had bow and arrows, now they have revolvers." Ryan: "That's what I meant, they have revolvers." Dalton: "They have revolvers?" Ryan: "Yes." Dalton: "Then what happened?" Ryan: "Then they shot us."

Dalton, who was trying to follow along with Ryan's story, reaches a point where he can't pretend anymore, as the narrative has become nonsensical. Following this exchange, Ryan would change his story once again, suggesting that they didn't shoot him; they only shot Heather. According to him, they put him in a sleeper hold. However, when Dalton inquired about the sleeper hold, Ryan claimed not to know what it meant. Eventually, Ryan abandoned the sleeper hold narrative and reverted back to the Richie and his father version, asserting that they entered and shot both of them. At this juncture, Ryan's story had become so convoluted and changed so frequently that it had become entirely unbelievable. Dalton, who had been attempting to follow Ryan's story, reached a point where he could no longer feign understanding, as the narrative had become incomprehensible.

Dalton: "You're telling me you're all over the board here, number one. You're saying bows and arrows, you're saying revolvers, and you're saying some other thing, and then you're saying they shot you in the eye. Okay, they shot you with a revolver in your eye?" Ryan: "Yes." Dalton: "And that's it, a bb gun?" Ryan: "No, it was a real gun, man. It was just a revolver." Dalton: "If they shot you in the eye with a revolver, you wouldn't be talking to me right now." Ryan: "How do you know?" Dalton: "Because most likely you'd be dead." Ryan: "That's what I thought too, man. I really don't know." Dalton: "So, you got shot first, and what happened? Did you fall to the ground?" Ryan: "Yeah, I was trying to get up, and I couldn't. I don't know..." Dalton: "And then she got shot?" Ryan: "Mm-hmm." Dalton: "And what... why... what did you do?" Ryan: "Nothing." Dalton: "Did you call 911?" Ryan: "Uh-uh." Dalton: "Did you see if she was still alive?" Ryan: "She was sleeping still, and that's it. I just let her sleep." Dalton: "She got shot in the side of the face, and you let her sleep?" Ryan: "Yes." Dalton: "This does not make any sense, Ryan."

After this exchange, Dalton shifts into a more aggressive approach, openly accusing Ryan of shooting and killing Heather. Ryan, however, continues to deny any involvement and maintains that he doesn't know anything about it. His responses are chaotic, contradictory, and lack coherence. Nothing he says seems to align, and the situation becomes increasingly perplexing.

Finally, at around 5:52 AM, approximately 45 minutes into the interrogation, Dalton reaches a point of frustration. Despite his belief that Ryan is responsible, none of Ryan's statements have effectively implicated him in the crime. Everything Ryan has uttered is a jumble of incomprehensible and inconsistent details, leaving Dalton uncertain about how to proceed.

In this moment of uncertainty, Dalton notices something on Ryan's face. "Look at it. Let me see your nose. Put your legs down, put your legs down. And bring your face closer," Dalton instructs. "Ow, my head hurts," Ryan responds.

"Okay, yeah. Be right back," Dalton

replies. This abrupt shift in focus leads to a pause in the interrogation as Dalton briefly leaves the room to consult with another officer.

What Dalton had finally discovered were four bullet holes in Ryan's face and head. Ryan had committed no crime; he was a victim, just as Heather had been. However, somehow Ryan had survived the attack that occurred on December 23rd. Two days before the welfare check, two men attempted to break into Ryan and Heather's house. These men were 23-year-old Richie Carver and his 54-year-old father, Larry Carver – the same Richie and Richie's father that Ryan had mentioned during the interrogation.

They were there because of an altercation that had occurred between Richie and the couple about a month earlier. At that time, Richie was actually living with Ryan and Heather. However, he began hitting on Heather, which upset her. Heather told Ryan about it, and he confronted Richie. This led to a big fight, and ultimately, Ryan kicked Richie out of the house. This incident infuriated Richie and embarrassed him.

So, on December 23rd, Richie and his

father were there to carry out their revenge plot. When they reached the back of Ryan and Heather's house, Ryan saw them at the back door through a glass door near the kitchen. He tried to stop them from getting inside, but Richie and Larry managed to barely open the door. Richie reached in with a gun and shot Ryan point-blank twice in the face.

The first bullet went in through Ryan's nose and exited the other side, creating the first two bullet holes. Then the bullet reversed its path, re-entering his head through his left eye and lodging in his brain. This created the third bullet hole, along with six pieces of his skull breaking off and lodging in his brain as well. The second bullet fired into Ryan's head hit the side but didn't penetrate his skull, causing the fourth bullet hole.

Ryan fell to the ground unconscious, and the attackers assumed he was dead. They managed to force the door open completely, stepped inside, walked over Ryan's body, and entered the living room where Heather was. Richie walked up to her, put a gun to her head, and fired a single shot. After she fell to the ground, the two men stole some items from the house and fled the scene. Ultimately, they would get caught, and both are currently serving life sentences.

It's believed Heather died instantly from her gunshot wound, but Ryan didn't. At some point, maybe a couple of hours after being shot, he woke up, though he had severe brain damage and wouldn't have known what was happening. He saw his girlfriend Heather lying on the couch but thought she was just sleeping. He went to his bedroom and fell asleep again. The next morning, on Christmas Eve, he woke up, still unaware of the situation. He spent that day wandering around the house with Heather's lifeless body on the couch.

Similarly, on Christmas Day, Ryan continued aimlessly wandering around the house, still believing Heather was sleeping. The welfare check was eventually called, and the police arrived. Upon seeing Ryan's bruised face and jumping to conclusions, they assumed he must have killed Heather. Rather than seeking medical attention for his facial wound, they thought it was a result of Heather resisting before he killed her.

Ryan sat in the police car outside the property for six hours without receiving any medical care, causing irreversible brain damage due to internal bleeding. Upon arriving at the police station, Ryan still didn't receive medical attention. Instead, he was interrogated for nearly two more hours despite having obvious facial injuries. Towards the end of the interrogation, Dalton stepped back and noticed the bullet holes on Ryan's face, particularly the one in his nose. This realization led to calling an ambulance, acknowledging the serious mistake that had been made.

Ryan was ultimately rushed to the hospital, where he underwent emergency surgery that saved his life. However, this came at a great cost. Not only did they have to remove a sizeable portion of his brain, but they also had to remove both of his eyes. After the surgery, Ryan was no longer independent. His brain damage was severe, rendering him unable to care for himself. Consequently, he had to move back in with his parents, who became his full-time caretakers.

Ten years later, Ryan passed away due to a seizure directly linked to the injuries he sustained from that attack. This tragic outcome was also connected to the lack of care he received during those critical initial eight hours after the police found him. When the mishandling of Ryan's case by the Phoenix Police Department became known, they conducted an internal investigation. However, no one was publicly disciplined as a result.

Regarding Ryan's family, they could have pursued a lawsuit against the Phoenix Police Department for their mishandling of the case. Yet, they chose not to take this route, stating that their only desire was to have their son back, something a lawsuit could never provide.

"UNFATHOMABLE CAPTIVITY: THE CHILLING ABDUCTION OF JAYME CLOSS"

If this case were to be adapted into a movie, its premise might strain belief. The perpetrator, devoid of any apparent motive and with a clean history devoid of serious crimes, commits such heinous acts, standing far apart from the typical cinematic villain. The narrative, centering around the targeting of a child and thereby intensifying the brutality, deviates from the familiar archetypes that audiences are accustomed to. The notion of a seemingly motiveless predator randomly singling out children is deeply unsettling; viewers anticipate motives, especially when innocent lives are at stake. Yet, in this instance, such motivation was conspicuously absent.

Even the perpetrator, during his time in prison, attempted to clarify his actions through a letter to the surviving family members of his victims. However, his explanation remained enigmatic and perplexing, lacking the compelling language necessary to convey the complex factors at play. He asserted that he was not a serial killer, yet his reasoning remained nebulous – a puzzle even to himself. The case remains unnerving, a portrayal of events orchestrated by an individual with no criminal background and seemingly no connection to the victims beyond a chance encounter.

Ultimately, it's a profoundly disturbing scenario that defies easy understanding, even by the person who perpetrated it.

In 2018, a 21-year-old named Jake Patterson was on his way to work at a Wisconsin cheese factory. He had only been working there for a few days, still getting used to his routine. It was just his third day on the job. Driving his Ford Taurus, he came to a stop behind a school bus, waiting as middle school kids got on. And in that moment, he saw her for the first time – a blonde-haired, green-eyed girl named Jayme Closs, who was only 13 years old. Little did anyone know, this unremarkable moment would lead to a chilling series of events.

As he sat in his car, Jake had a realization. He decided then and there that Jayme would be the girl he would abduct. Jake's plan involved careful forethought. He took his father's Mossberg 12-gauge shotgun, assuming its common use would make it hard to trace. He purchased a balaclava, shaving his head and beard to eliminate potential forensic evidence. He got gloves to avoid leaving prints, steel-toed boots for practicality, and dark clothing to blend in. He even disabled the trunk release inside his car, ensuring it could only be opened with the key. His attention to detail was unsettling.

The execution of his plan, however, proved to be more complicated. Jake made two unsuccessful attempts to abduct Jayme. On the first occasion, he saw cars in the driveway and was spooked, leaving without making a move. On the second, he was about to approach the house when lights came on, causing him to retreat once again.

On October 15, 2018, under unfortunate circumstances, Jake Patterson would succeed in his sinister plan. It was around midnight when he quietly rolled into the driveway of the Closs family's modest home. With his car lights off and headlights dimmed, he went unnoticed initially. Inside the house, 13-year-old Jayme Closs was sound asleep with her dog, Molly. However, Molly's barking alerted Jayme, who looked out her window to see an unfamiliar car. Sensing danger, she hurried to her parents' room to raise the alarm.

James Closs, Jayme's father, cautiously approached the front door, equipped only with a flashlight, while Jayme and her mother, Denise, sought refuge in the bathroom. An intuitive sense of danger prompted them to barricade the bathroom door with a dresser, huddled together in the bathtub with the curtains drawn tightly. James stood sentinel at the front door, engaging with Jake as he arrived, half-expecting an officer of the law. However, cruel irony took the reins as Jake aimed his shotgun and the trigger was pulled, extinguishing James' life in an instant.

In the confines of the bathroom, Jayme absorbed the shockwave of the shotgun blast, realizing her father was gone. Denise, her mother, acutely comprehended the severity of the situation and swiftly dialed 911 for help. Jake Patterson's determination crystallized as he wielded his shotgun to obliterate the doorknob, swiftly gaining entry. Methodically, he scoured the house, room by room, every door ajar except the one guarding Jayme and Denise.

Fueled by an undeniable compulsion, Jake shattered the bathroom's defenses, revealing Denise shielding Jayme. He demanded that Denise bind Jayme's hands and silence her, yet Denise resolutely refused, driven by a maternal instinct that eclipsed his demands. Jake took matters into his own hands, stifling Jayme's protests and wresting her freedom. A single deadly shot silenced Denise before he seized Jayme, forcefully placing her in the trunk of his car. In a matter of minutes, he asserted complete control.

Embarking on a drive of approximately

70 miles to his own house, Jake kept Jayme captive for the next three harrowing months. His swift and calculated actions left a trail of devastation and a terrified community in his wake. The narrative of that night etched into memory serves as a haunting reminder of the unfathomable depths darkness can descend to.

The entire community, along with investigators, was fervently searching for her. Yet, expectations of her safe return were low, given the grim statistics surrounding child abductions. Sadly, most cases like these don't culminate in the child's safe return. This growing national crisis focused everyone's attention on Jayme's disappearance but finding her seemed like an increasingly distant possibility.

During this harrowing period, Jayme found herself imprisoned in the cluttered and remote residence of Jake Patterson, nestled deep within the woods, far from the watchful eyes of the world. Upon her arrival at his hideaway, he meticulously eradicated any trace of her presence, incinerating her clothing, gloves, and the duct tape that bound her. In a grim and chilling turn, he replaced her clothes with his sister's pajamas before confining her beneath a bed in his dwelling, where she had nothing but a pillow and a blanket.

Having been a firsthand witness to the brutal slaying of her parents, Jayme grasped the dire gravity of her situation. With an iron grip on her existence, Jake Patterson ominously warned her of the dire consequences awaiting her should she dare to escape. The haunting specter of her parents' tragic demise lingered in her psyche, forcing her into compliance with his every command. She endured interminable stretches of time, often spanning 8 to 12 hours, concealed beneath the bed, stripped of the most basic necessities for survival.

For the initial two weeks, Jake remained vigilant, claiming to have a shotgun positioned just outside her door, ready to thwart any police intervention. As the days passed without any sign of the authorities, his confidence grew. He even began inviting guests over, instructing Jayme to stay hidden in her room during these visits. For 87 days, she endured this harrowing existence, isolated and neglected, grappling with her grief and loss while hidden beneath the bed.

Only on one occasion did Jake leave the house, ostensibly to visit a grandparent, but he made it abundantly clear that attempting to escape would result in severe consequences. Evidently growing overconfident that he had evaded capture, he even applied for a job, briefly leaving the house for an interview, seemingly aiming to return to a semblance of normalcy.

As he departed that morning, Jayme lay beneath the bed, overcome by an intense surge of determination. She understood that she couldn't endure captivity any further. With swift resolve, she pushed aside the makeshift barricade of weights and clothing, rallying her final reservoir of strength. Her captor's absence created an opening for escape that she couldn't ignore. Seizing the opportunity, she emerged from her hiding place, hurriedly donning his oversized shoes, even managing to place them on the wrong feet in her haste.

Without a clear sense of direction or location, she bolted through the door, propelled by desperation and an unwavering determination to liberate herself from the clutches of captivity.

Around 4 P.M., a woman named Jeannie Nutter was walking her dog in the area. Her keen instincts told her that something was amiss as she spotted a coatless, gloveless teenager approaching her. It was bitterly cold, and this encounter was far from ordinary. Instinctively, Jeannie sensed the urgency and recognized the girl's dire situation. As the teenager drew closer, uttering the words, "I'm lost, I need help, my name is Jayme," Jeannie immediately realized who she was – the missing Jayme Closs. Overwhelmed with emotion, she enveloped Jayme in a warm embrace, reassuring her that she was safe now.

Guiding Jayme to a nearby neighbor's house, Jeannie introduced her to the homeowners and conveyed, "This is Jayme Closs, we need to call the police." The homeowners, armed and ready, formed a protective circle around Jayme, as Jeannie dialed the police, urgently stressing the need for immediate assistance. The police were momentarily stunned by the news of Jayme's discovery, struggling to comprehend the gravity of the situation. However, the urgency of the situation finally registered, and they dispatched officers to the scene.

As each moment ticked by, the fear that her captor might realize her absence only heightened, turning Jayme's rescue into a race against time. Fortunately, the police arrived promptly, ensuring Jayme's safety. Although her emotional wounds would require time to heal, Jayme was at last physically liberated from the clutches of her captor.

Returning home from his pivotal job interview, Jake encountered an unsettling sight: Jayme was nowhere to be found, her footsteps imprinting a path in the snow leading away from his property. Filled with alarm, he embarked on a search, his panic driving him to scour the surroundings. However, the inexorable hand of fate intervened, and the police swiftly apprehended him. His car, his presence—everything pointed to his guilt. Upon being detained, he offered no resistance, promptly confirming his identity and culpability.

In the aftermath, Jake Patterson received a life sentence in prison, with any possibility of parole extinguished forever. As he serves his sentence, a chilling question lingers: how could such a heinous act unfold? The unsettling truth is that cases like these resist logical explanation. Our comprehension of human behavior leads us to seek understandable motives behind such crimes. We instinctively look for a rationale that aligns with our understanding. However, Jayme's harrowing experience defies such rationality. The concept that a seemingly unrelated stranger could arbitrarily choose a child, brutally murder her parents in her presence, and keep her imprisoned for no apparent reason, without any prior criminal history, is a disturbing puzzle. It defies our typical patterns of reasoning and comprehension. The unsettling reality remains that sometimes, however incomprehensible, such events simply occur, challenging our fundamental understanding of humanity and the depths of human behavior.

"PIGGY PALACE NIGHTMARE: THE DISTURBING CRIMES OF ROBERT PICKTON"

If you have heard of Piggy Palace, the focus of today's story, then you know how horrific this story is. If you've never heard of Piggy Palace, well, reader discretion is advised.

Robert Pickton was born in 1949 in Port Coquitlam in British Columbia, which is about 15 miles to the east of Vancouver. He, along with his brother and sister, was raised by their parents on a big pig farm. In the 1970s, their parents passed away, and so the property was handed down to them. Robert and his brother took over the daily operations of the farm, while their sister decided to just move away.

Over the next couple of decades, Robert and his brother attempted to run the pig farm, but pretty quickly they stopped taking care of it, and it fell into decline. Neighbor's and visitors recalled seeing the pigs that were still there free roaming the property. As for the brothers, it appeared they had just stopped bathing, and despite walking all day in mud and pig feces, it seemed like they never took off their boots when they went inside.

One of the few farm workers that stayed with the Pickton's through the farm's decline was a guy by the name of Bill Hiscox, and he said the farm was a really creepy place. He also mentioned that Robert was a really creepy guy who was prone to just totally bizarre behavior, even though he didn't smoke, drink, or use any substances.

Eventually, the Pickton brothers realized they were not cut out to run the pig farm as their family had for generations before them. They decided that their best move was to sell portions of their land, but neither of them could have guessed just how much their land was worth. From 1994 to 1995, they managed to sell off almost all of their property to an urban developer for over 5 million dollars. Suddenly, these filthy, failed pig farmers had become millionaires, and neither of them knew what to do with the money.

After a year of just sitting on the money and not doing much with it, they decided they wanted to do some good with their newfound wealth. In 1996, they established an official charity called the Piggy Palace Good Times Society. The charity's purpose, at least on paper, was to help raise money for various organizations that they deemed worthy by running events like dances and shows. While that might have been their original intention for this charity, what it ultimately became was a guise to host wild, drug, and alcohol-fueled parties inside their slaughterhouse.

Even though the slaughterhouse wasn't being used anymore because they were no longer really involved in pig farming, it still conspicuously had big hooks coming down from the ceiling and blood stains all over the ground underneath them. These Piggy Palace parties became infamous in Coquitlam, drawing crowds of up to 2000 people, predominantly bikers, drug addicts, and prostitutes from the poverty-stricken Downtown East side of Vancouver. Robert had become familiar with that part of Vancouver because he used to go through there all the time to dispose of animal waste products at their rendering plant. Once the Piggy Palace charity was in full swing, Robert started venturing back into the neighborhood, cruising down the 10-block strip known as the low track, attempting to recruit people for his parties. Most of those he recruited were downtrodden women who, in dire circumstances, agreed to attend these parties in exchange for food, money, drugs, and alcohol.

Simultaneously, as Robert conducted his recruiting campaign, women from the Downtown East side started disappearing in alarming numbers. These vanishings caught the attention of both men and women in the area, although they refrained from reporting them due to a deep-seated distrust of the police and authority figures in general. However, as the tally of missing women steadily grew, whispers of a serial killer operating within the vicinity began to spread.

In response to the unsettling atmosphere, residents became more cautious, venturing outside only in groups and maintaining vigilant watch for anything unusual – unfamiliar people, out-of-place vehicles, or any irregularities in the neighborhood. Despite these heightened security measures, the alarming rate of women disappearing continued unabated, leaving the community in a state of collective anxiety and confusion.

When the police were eventually notified about the concerning number of missing women, their reaction was lackluster, to say the least. As no bodies had been found, the police argued it was reasonable to assume that the women's lifestyles had caught up with them, suggesting they might have run away or succumbed to drug-related issues. However, despite the insistence of Downtown East side residents that something more sinister was at play, the police chose not to engage, dismissing the concerns.

Criticism swiftly descended upon the police force once news of their apathetic response reached the newspapers. Many accused them of deliberately downplaying the urgency of the situation, believing that the missing women, predominantly drug addicts and prostitutes, were not receiving the full attention of an investigation they deserved. The police, though, rejected these accusations and maintained their stance.

On the evening of March 22nd, 1997— exactly one year after the inception of Piggy Palace and the commencement of their raucous parties— and after a year had passed with dozens of women disappearing from the Downtown East side— the Pickton brothers' neighbor was startled by a frantic knock on their front door. Reacting swiftly, they rushed to answer the door and were confronted with the sight of a woman, hunched over and clutching her bleeding stomach. Dangling from her wrist was a handcuff, an alarming and bewildering sight that left the neighbor utterly shocked.

Despite their shock, the neighbor quickly guided the injured woman inside and promptly summoned an ambulance. The woman was swiftly transported to the hospital, where she underwent emergency surgery to address her injuries.

After undergoing emergency surgery and beginning her recovery, the woman, who identified herself as Wendy, recounted her ordeal to the nurses. She revealed that she had been at a Piggy Palace party hosted by Robert Pickton, one of the farm's owners. During the event, Robert had attempted to handcuff her, leading to a struggle. In the midst of the struggle, he had drawn a knife and stabbed her in the stomach. Wendy managed to wrest the knife from him, subsequently stabbing him in the face. She then fled the scene, seeking refuge at the neighbor's house.

Coincidentally, Robert Pickton arrived at the same hospital shortly thereafter, sporting a facial laceration consistent with a stabbing. Hospital staff had already alerted the police, who promptly arrived at the scene. Upon searching Robert, the police discovered a handcuff key in one of his pockets, which successfully opened the handcuff still attached to Wendy's wrist. This evidence led to Robert's arrest on charges of attempted murder.

While in custody, Robert offered an alternate version of events. He claimed that Wendy, a drug addict, had attempted to rob him at one of his Piggy Palace parties. According to his account, a confrontation escalated into a struggle during which both parties were injured. The police chose to believe his story, dropping all charges and releasing him.

Upon returning to the farm, Robert's actions aroused suspicion in Bill Hiscox, the sole remaining worker for the Pickton brothers. Having learned of the numerous missing women from the Downtown East side, Bill harbored concerns about Robert's involvement. Knowing that Robert frequently brought women back from the area for his parties, Bill felt something was amiss. After grappling with his intuition for several months, Bill decided to take action. He contacted the Crime Stoppers tip line, sharing his belief that Robert had attacked Wendy, not the other way around. Furthermore, he voiced his suspicion that Robert might be connected to the missing women cases.

Bill also disclosed that a recent female guest at the farm had observed a pile of women's clothing, along with numerous purses and women's identification cards inside Robert's trailer. However, when the police attempted to corroborate this information with the guest, named Lisa, she hesitated due to fear of Robert and refused to cooperate. As a result of lacking Lisa's testimony, the police were unable to secure a search warrant to delve further into the matter. Thus, the police gradually lost focus on the case and shifted their attention to other investigations.

Throughout the following years, the Pickton's persistently organized these grand Piggy Palace parties, undeterred despite city authorities' eventual intervention and attempts to shut them down. Amidst this backdrop, a disconcerting trend materialized: multiple women continued to vanish from the downtown East side, their cases receiving minimal police scrutiny. Bill, steadfast in his determination, persistently sounded the alarm by voicing his suspicions about Robert Pickton's possible connection to these disappearances.

Finally, in 2002, a former employee of the Pickton farm stepped forward and provided crucial information to the police. He revealed that he had personally witnessed illegal weapons inside Robert's trailer. This revelation was sufficient for the police to obtain a search warrant, and in February of that year, they executed the search, discovering the illicit firearms and various items directly linked to some of the missing women from the downtown east side.

Following these developments, Robert was arrested once more and later released on bail under strict surveillance conditions. He was also forbidden from returning to the farm while a comprehensive search was conducted. During this meticulous investigation, a significant breakthrough emerged: traces of one of the missing women's blood were discovered inside Robert's trailer. Consequently, he was re-arrested and faced murder charges.

While in custody, Robert shared his cell with an individual he believed to be another detainee. Unbeknownst to him, however, this individual was an undercover police officer, and their conversations were discreetly recorded.

In the wake of these conversations,

Robert gradually divulged his darkest secrets to the undercover officer, admitting that he had been disposing of the victims' bodies in a rendering plant.

Subsequently, Robert confessed to the shocking revelation of killing 49 people, a substantial number of whom constituted the missing women from the downtown east side. After a thorough investigation, it was determined that Robert's spree of killings commenced in 1991, gaining momentum in 1996 when he and his brother initiated the Piggy Palace gatherings. These events facilitated a faster process of luring victims to the farm, where he would then employ various sinister methods.

Once the victims were on his property, Robert would entice them into his trailer, where he would handcuff them, declare their fate sealed, and then administer fatal doses of antifreeze or strangle them to death. Subsequently, he would transport the bodies to the slaughterhouse, where they would be gruesomely dismembered. A significant portion of the victims' remains were fed to the pigs, while the remaining parts were transported to a rendering plant in the downtown east side, close to where the victims were likely abducted.

A rendering plant processes animal waste products, grinding them down to create a gelatine that finds its way into various everyday items, including cosmetics and candies, such as lipstick and gummy bears. Amid this horrifying disposal process, Robert would occasionally set aside select cuts of meat, grinding them with pork to produce sausages. Shockingly, these sausages were served at the Piggy Palace parties, distributed to neighbor's, food banks, and orphanages.

After excavating the Pickton farm, meticulously examining 300,000 cubic meters of soil and pig waste, investigators discovered fragments of remains from 26 women. Consequently, Robert was charged with all 26 murders, although only six led to convictions due to a lack of concrete evidence. He received a life sentence in prison, where he remains to this day. Notably, his brother and sister were never implicated or charged in connection with these heinous crimes.

"Beneath the Depths: The Tragic Tale of the Kursk Submarine"

In the year 2000, a handwritten note was discovered at the bottom of the ocean within the Arctic Circle, revealing an utterly horrifying true story.

On the morning of August 12, 2000, 33 of Russia's finest naval warships halted within a specific section of the Barren Sea. This sea, an 800-mile stretch of freezing water in the Arctic Circle just northwest of Russia, was the location chosen for a massive military training exercise. The purpose was to run through various war game scenarios. For instance, one ship would simulate an enemy combatant, while the other ships practiced targeting and firing at it. Of course, real missiles or torpedoes wouldn't be used—only non-exploding duds.

Around 9 AM, Admiral Popov, the head of the operation, who was on board one of the 33 ships, authorized a submarine to fire two dummy torpedoes at a designated target—an "enemy" ship, which was actually another vessel among the 33. This marked the commencement of the multi-day exercise. Throughout the day and night, they engaged in these war game scenarios.

By the next morning, 24 hours into the exercise, Admiral Popov took a break from the action to speak with Russian reporters via phone. During this interview, he assured them that the training exercise was progressing precisely as planned and appeared poised for significant success. However, a problem arose simultaneously. While Admiral Popov spoke optimistically to the reporters, family members of some of the crews involved in the exercise caught wind of a rumor. This unverified information suggested that something had gone awry with one of the ships. Lacking further details, these concerned family members began calling the naval base, seeking clarification.

Initially, the phone operator on the base dismissed these inquiries, stating that they had heard nothing amiss and there were no issues. Yet, inadvertently, the operator hinted that they too had heard the rumor and suspected it might be true. As the worried family members pushed for more information, the operator grew reticent, claiming an inability to provide additional details. Subsequently, a family member who had received this partial confirmation contacted the media and shared the unfolding situation.

The media swiftly approached Admiral Popov, seeking his response to the rumor. He chose not to address the media's queries, which paradoxically offered a measure of reassurance to the families of the crews. They believed that if Admiral Popov continued the exercise seemingly unaffected, then the rumor might hold less weight.

For the remainder of that Sunday, family members and the media remained in a state of uncertainty, awaiting any potential updates since there was little else they could do in the absence of concrete information.

On the following day, Monday the 14th, which marked 48 hours after the commencement of the training exercise, significant news emerged. Russian officials appeared on TV to address the rumor that had been circulating. They confirmed that something did indeed occur during the exercise. The incident involved the Kursk, one of the submarines among the 33 ships participating in the exercise. The Kursk had encountered minor technical challenges, which led to the submarine being grounded at the bottom of the Barren Sea. However, the officials emphasized that this situation was routine and under control. They assured the public that communication with the submarine was ongoing through radio, the crew members were safe, and efforts were underway to supply air and power to the vessel. The officials conveyed confidence that the submarine would soon resurface, urging everyone not to worry.

Naturally, family members of the Kursk's crew were fraught with panic upon hearing this news. Despite the government's outward confidence, their own confidence in the safety of their loved ones was not assured. Despite these concerns, the families held onto the knowledge that the Kursk was an extraordinary and exceptionally secure submarine. It was, in fact, considered Russia's most advanced vessel, built with meticulous attention to detail and equipped with cutting-edge technology. The submarine was constructed using specialized, heavily reinforced steel capable of withstanding direct torpedo impacts without grave damage. Furthermore, its interior was fitted with state-of-the-art amenities. Given the circumstances, if one had to be trapped at the ocean floor inside a submarine, the Kursk was the best option available. This realization provided some solace to the families.

However, despite the government's repeated assurances through news outlets that the situation was minor, and that the Kursk would soon be recovered, the submarine remained submerged over the subsequent days. The lack of new information from the government deepened the void of knowledge, leading to growing anxiety among the families and speculation within the media. As days passed without progress, the families grew increasingly worried, and the media started to question the veracity of the government's narrative. Was the Kursk's situation truly the result of minor technical difficulties, as the government asserted, or was it something graver? This uncertainty persisted until August 21st when the truth would finally come to light.

Nine days after the commencement of the training exercise, a Norwegian dive team, present to assist in the recovery operation, managed to descend to the Kursk. They succeeded in entering the submarine through an escape hatch—a water-tight compartment on the submarine's exterior that facilitates entry and exit without flooding the vessel. Once within the Kursk, these Norwegian divers were profoundly taken aback by what they encountered.

While the intricate details of the events inside the Kursk continue to be debated, one aspect of the story enjoys a near-universal consensus: the occurrences within Compartment Number Nine. The Kursk was divided into nine watertight sections, sequentially numbered from the foremost bow to the farthest stern. Dmitry Kolesnikov, a 27-year-old crew member of the Kursk, provides an illuminating account of the crucial events that unfolded within Compartment Number Nine. His testimony serves as a pivotal guide in understanding these events.

Dimitri was born into a family of submariners. His father and his father's father were both submariners. Dimitri idolized them, and his childhood aspiration was to follow in their footsteps. In the late 1990s, his dream materialized when he joined the Russian Navy as a commissioned naval officer. His orders led him to serve aboard the Kursk. Approximately four months prior to the training exercise in the Barren Sea, Dimitri encountered Olga, a high school teacher, whom he swiftly married.

Shortly after their wedding, Dimitri arranged for Olga to visit the Kursk for a tour. Equipped with a video camera, Olga documented her exploration of the ship. On the footage, Dimitri can be seen with an ever-present smile, eagerly guiding her through the vessel, introducing her to his colleagues, and revealing the ship's confined spaces. The video unmistakably captures Dimitri's immense pride in his job, as well as his enthusiasm for sharing this facet of his life with his wife.

Fast forward to August 12, 2000—Dimitri and 117 fellow crew members on the Kursk arrived at their designated area in the Barren Sea for the training exercise. At 11:27 AM, the captain of the Kursk communicated over the radio with Admiral Popov, who was aboard a different ship at the time. The captain informed the admiral that the Kursk was about to launch its two dummy torpedoes.

Subsequently, activity commenced in the first compartment of the Kursk, where torpedoes—both real and simulated—were stored. These two dummy torpedoes were being loaded. Meanwhile, Dimitri, stationed all the way in the seventh compartment (the engine room, where he was in charge of the personnel working there), was coordinating his team. As the loading progressed, with dials being adjusted and levers pulled, a sudden and thunderous crash erupted. The ship convulsed and then violently careened to one side, as though savagely seized by an unseen force at its front.

What Dimitri and the men in the seventh compartment couldn't possibly have known was that one of the actual torpedoes in the first compartment had malfunctioned and detonated. However, due to the robust construction of the Kursk, the strength of its outer walls prevented the torpedo from puncturing through. It did cause substantial damage and ignited a massive fire. Nevertheless, the sub remained afloat.

Back in the seventh compartment, the jolted and disoriented Dimitri stood up from being knocked to the ground. Amid the blaring alarms and rampant chaos, he assumed control of the situation. He instructed his men to follow the emergency protocol, which entailed sealing the watertight doors of their compartment. Dimitri, in this instance, sealed both doors—the one leading to the sixth compartment and the other to the eighth. This practice aimed to safeguard against flooding in case of leaks elsewhere within the submarine.

As Dimitri and his team sealed the doors, they would have witnessed and smelled the encroaching smoke as it infiltrated through the ventilation ducts. The uncontrolled fire was now raging at the submarine's forefront. Simultaneously, they felt the submarine abruptly tilt upward at an intense angle. The captain was struggling to surface. However, before they could break through, the uncontrolled blaze reached the live torpedoes, setting off an instantaneous chain reaction of explosions.

The subsequent series of explosions tragically resulted in the loss of almost all individuals located in the front half of the submarine. As the walls were breached by the second explosion, icy Arctic water flooded the vessel. For those who had not succumbed to the initial explosion, the threat of drowning became an immediate and grim reality. At this point the sole survivors were likely those in the sixth, seventh, eighth, and ninth compartments, situated towards the rear.

Dimitri and the men in the seventh compartment endured the substantial impact of the second explosion, which rattled the submarine and threw them about. Despite their shaken state, they remained alive, acutely aware of the dire circumstances. Presumably, they clung to any available fixtures as the submarine, bereft of its control tower, plunged downward. At precisely 11:32 AM, a mere four minutes after the initial blast, the Kursk slammed nose-first into the ocean floor 350 feet below the surface. Subsequently, the aft portion of the Kursk settled down.

The details of the subsequent two hours aboard the Kursk, following its collision with the ocean floor, remain uncertain. However, certain aspects are clear. The submarine retained power, providing internal illumination. Additionally, the air purifiers continued to function, making breathing relatively tolerable despite the smoke and chemical fumes. At some point, Dimitri and his fellow compartment occupants must have detected sounds emanating from the sixth compartment. Recall that they had sealed both the eighth and the sixth compartment doors. Deviating from protocol, Dimitri chose to open the door leading to the sixth compartment, allowing any surviving crew members to enter their space. Upon opening the door and peering into the sixth compartment, they would have observed rapid flooding.

By 1:30 p.m., those forward of the sixth compartment were already deceased. Dimitri, along with his comrades from the seventh compartment and the survivors from the sixth, was compelled to retreat sequentially through the eighth and finally into the ninth compartment due to the relentless flooding. Although they had initially sealed their watertight doors, the explosion had rendered the walls non-watertight. Shrapnel from the explosion had pierced the walls, creating breaches. Thus, closing the watertight doors proved futile over time. As one compartment filled, water leaked through the damaged walls. This awareness would have been acutely present to Dimitri and his fellow survivors. Upon reaching the ninth compartment, situated at the rearmost part of the submarine, they faced an inescapable predicament. The inexorable advance of water would ultimately drown them, leaving them with only the prospect of rescue or escape via the hatch.

Despite the undeniably horrifying nature of their circumstances, Dimitri maintained an astonishing level of composure. So composed, in fact, that he retrieved a sheet of paper amidst the confines of the ninth compartment, where he was accompanied by 22 other individuals. Upon this paper, he carefully noted the date and time in a corner, before methodically recounting the unfolding events. His account detailed the explosion and the grim realization that he and his companions were likely the sole survivors. Their confinement within the ninth compartment was acknowledged, as was their reliance on eventual rescue. Dimitri also referenced the consideration of using the escape hatch, which seemingly had proven ineffective.

Having penned this organized and legible entry, Dimitri meticulously folded the paper and tucked it into his pocket. An hour and a half later, an abrupt loss of power plunged them into deep obscurity, an abyss of pitch-blackness. Simultaneously, plummeting temperatures exacerbated their plight. Yet the most harrowing development was the slow encroachment of water through the breached walls. Aware that their refuge would inevitably succumb to the rising tide, Dimitri acted. Retrieving the paper from his pocket, he added to his earlier account. This time, his handwriting wavered, rendered nearly illegible by the trembling of hypothermia. His words bore witness to the enveloping darkness—Dimitri indicated he was writing blindly due to the total absence of light. In this second note, bearing a timestamp an hour and a half subsequent to the first, Dimitri candidly expressed doubt about his survival. The note's content, shared by all its authors, conveyed their collective resignation to their fate. Amid the increasing deluge and the chilling surroundings, Dimitri composed a heartfelt message to his beloved wife and family, bidding them a final farewell. His closing words, "Regards to everybody, no need to despair," left an indelible imprint.

Having inscribed these farewell words, Dimitri carefully refolded the paper and placed it within his breast pocket. Enshrouded in darkness, accompanied by the disconcerting rush of water, Dimitri and his 22 companions braced themselves for the inevitable, ready to meet their fate.

The exact duration of Dimitri's survival, along with the 22 other men in Compartment 9, remains unknown. Experts speculate that the entire Kursk submarine was fully inundated approximately 8 hours after the initial explosion. One of the most poignant aspects of this tragedy is the potential for salvation if the Russian response had been swifter and better coordinated. Despite two ships, including the vessel carrying Admiral Popov, sensing the force of the Kursk's second explosion, no immediate action was taken. Though reports were filed, they did not translate into significant intervention.

Moreover, when communication with the Kursk faltered after the presumed launch of the dummy torpedoes, a casual assumption persisted that radio malfunctions were to blame, leading to the erroneous belief that the crew remained unharmed. It wasn't until later that evening that the Russian Navy realized the gravity of the situation, acknowledging the Kursk's disappearance. Subsequently, hours passed before a rescue submersible was dispatched to the submarine's location. Even upon reaching the site, efforts to establish a connection with the escape hatch proved fruitless, leaving any potential survivors stranded without access to the rescue submersible.

In the ensuing days, Russia grappled with the challenging endeavor of accessing the submarine, initially refusing foreign assistance from Norway, America, and Great Britain. Only after nine days had passed since the Kursk's sinking did Russia finally accept foreign aid, prompting a Norwegian dive team to venture forth to open the escape hatch. Inside the submarine, they encountered a somber scene—its chambers submerged, lifeless bodies drifting. Among the casualties was Dimitri, his motionless form holding the poignant note tucked in his breast pocket.

Following this tragedy, Russia posthumously honored the entire Kursk crew with the Order of Courage, a significant military distinction. Additionally, the families of the crew were granted a stipend equivalent to ten years of salary. They were also provided with complimentary housing in any Russian city, while the expenses for their children's college education were covered.

"TWISTED JOURNEY: UNRAVELLING THE ENIGMA OF JULIAN AND CAROLYN'S ABDUCTION"

Back in 2008, a young man found himself navigating a dirt road meandering through a dense forest. Amid the backdrop, a sizable creature caught his attention up ahead. Lying motionless at the roadside, this unfamiliar entity piqued his curiosity. Determined to uncover its identity, he carefully drove past the inert form, eventually halting his car. Stepping out, he retraced his path, his footsteps carrying him back toward the puzzling creature.

Drawing closer, he crouched down to obtain a clearer view of the creature's features. In the midst of his scrutiny, an unsettling sound reached his ears, originating from the area behind him. A disconcerting sense of foreboding accompanied this auditory disturbance. Abruptly, before he could pivot to address the source of the sound, everything plunged into darkness.

In the year 2008, a 22-year-old named Julian Buchwald found himself residing in the tranquil expanse of Budgery, a quaint rural town nestled in Southern Australia. This hamlet served as his family's abode, encompassing a sprawling 1200-acre domain—equivalent to around two square miles. Yet, this vast expanse was predominantly blanketed in dense underbrush and forested terrain, curtailing their excursions primarily to the immediate vicinity of their residence.

A mere 20-minute drive north of Budgery lay the quaint village of Churchill. In this peaceful locale, Julian's romantic interest, Carolyn Watson, resided with her family. The story of Julian and Carolyn, a devoted couple, began with a fortuitous encounter at a shared place of worship two years prior. United by their strong Christian faith, they shared a mutual devotion and dreams of a future together. Their aspirations included the prospect of marriage, with plans to solidify their commitment the following year when Carolyn celebrated her 18th birthday—an event that would also mark the completion of her studies.

The story begins on Tuesday, March 4th, as Julian and Carolyn, captivated by the enchanting beauty of nature, decided to enjoy a picnic lunch together. They selected the idyllic waterfall nestled within Julian's family estate as their meeting spot. Under the morning sun, Julian drove his family car, heading to Churchill to pick up Carolyn. Subsequently, they embarked on the journey back to Julian's family haven, following a dirt road that wound through the lush forest.

During this voyage, Julian's gaze was drawn ahead to a peculiar sight—a sizable, unfamiliar creature lay lifeless by the roadside. Intrigued by this mysterious spectacle, Julian's curiosity drove him to halt the car momentarily and venture towards the enigmatic creature. Leaping out of the car, he approached the beast, which appeared to be lifeless. As Julian studied it, an unsettling rustle reached his ears from behind, raising his alertness. Swiftly, before he could pivot and address this auditory intrusion, darkness consumed his consciousness.

In the interim, Carolyn, seated in the car, noted the passage of time, her anticipation mounting as Julian's return was delayed. Annoyance eventually morphed into concern, prompting her to exit the car and investigate. Stepping out, she directed her gaze down the dirt road Julian had ventured along, intending to ascertain his whereabouts. However, her glance was arrested by an unthinkable sight—a presence in the midst of the road, inexplicable and fear-inducing. Abject terror rooted her to the spot as the unidentifiable entity advanced towards her.

Around 3:30 PM, the day's unfolding events captured the attention of Julian's mother. The noticeable delay in her son's return stirred a sense of unease within her, prompting her to venture out onto the porch and await his return. With each passing minute devoid of Julian's appearance, her worry escalated. Eying the clock, she noted the impending 3 PM deadline they had promised their families.

Julian's mother shifted her attention toward the driveway that led to their property. However, her focus was momentarily diverted by a curious sight—a plastic bottle wedged in the fence. Intrigued, she took a closer look, ultimately discovering a note concealed within the bottle. The message within seemed to be addressed to her or her family, shedding light on the events that had transpired during Julian and Carolyn's day.

And so, the narrative continues to unfold—a tapestry woven from the threads of idyllic Australian countryside, youthful romance, and an enigmatic note that held the promise of unravelling the mystery shrouding the day's curious events.

As the story progresses, it reveals unsettling details that lie beneath the surface. The note, discovered amidst the beauty of the countryside, bore eerie and cryptic symbols intertwined with a sinister message. The unsettling ambiance created by these satanic symbols, combined with the note's incomprehensible language marred by egregious grammatical errors, painted a disturbing picture. The chilling message was glaringly clear—the note conveyed that the young couple, Julian and Carolyn, referred to only as "the boy" and "the girl," had fallen into the clutches of the ONA cult. Moreover, the note ominously mandated that the family refrain from involving law enforcement. In return, Julian and Carolyn's safety would ostensibly be assured. However, the message, laden with dread, refrained from disclosing any specifics regarding their fate. Intriguingly, the note abstained from demanding a ransom, instead emphasizing the dire consequences of involving the authorities—an impending sense of terror if the police were summoned.

Overwhelmed by fear and paralyzed by indecision, Julian's mother found herself trapped in a nightmarish dilemma. The weight of the situation was suffocating, leaving her grappling with uncertainty about the most prudent course of action. Despite the looming threat to her family, the powerful maternal instinct to shield her children from harm drove her to make a choice. Ultimately, unable to ignore the compulsion to ensure her family's safety, she contacted the police, shattering the eerie silence that had blanketed their existence.

Responding promptly to the call, the police descended upon the property to scrutinize the alarming message that had thrust the family into turmoil. The note's contents bore a distinct trait—a series of cryptic, satanic symbols that adorned its surface. These symbols, emblematic of an unsettling belief system, heightened the note's menacing aura. The skewed grammar and disturbing imagery punctuating the message compounded its disturbing nature.

The initial response from the police leaned towards skepticism, considering the note as a potential hoax or prank. The brief period that had passed since Julian and Carolyn's disappearance, combined with the cryptic message in the bottle, created uncertainty about the presence of a darker conspiracy. However, beneath this initial doubt, a disquieting realization began to emerge, suggesting the possibility of more sinister circumstances at play.

However, as the hours turned into days, and Julian and Carolyn remained conspicuously absent, the police's skepticism began to wane. The note's eerie composition and its uncanny similarities to a previous message received by Carolyn's parents morphed from an oddity into a chilling puzzle piece. The police's preparations shifted from hopeful searches to somber contemplation of a bleaker scenario—one that hinted at the likelihood that Julian and Carolyn might no longer be among the living. The absence of further communication from the purported ONA cult deepened this sense of foreboding, casting a shadow over the escalating situation.

On March 11th, precisely seven days after Carolyn and Julian's mysterious disappearance, the narrative took an unexpected turn. Amidst the intricate web of events, a farmer found himself driving along a winding back road nestled within the rugged expanse of Alpine National Park. The serenity of the surroundings was disrupted as the farmer's gaze fixed upon a perplexing sight up ahead. Two young individuals, barely clad in clothing, emerged from the thick forest bordering the road. In an unanticipated twist, their disheveled figures slumped onto the roadside, casting an aura of vulnerability.

Driven by concern for their well-being, the farmer maneuvered his vehicle to a halt beside the duo. Lowering his window, he extended his inquiries, seeking assurance of their safety. Responding to his queries, Carolyn and Julian, the very individuals at the heart of the ongoing mystery, approached the vehicle, with urgency and desperation in their eyes, they introduced themselves and implored the farmer for aid.

Moved by their plight, the farmer extended his help, inviting them into his vehicle. His selfless act evolved into a journey to the nearest hospital, spurred by the urgency of their situation. The news of this unforeseen encounter reverberated through the law enforcement channels in Budgery. The revelation that Carolyn and Julian had been found and were, astonishingly, alive injected fresh determination into the investigation. Mobilizing swiftly, the police set out on a path towards the hospital adjacent to Alpine National Park.

Within the hospital's walls, conversations with medical professionals provided a glimpse into the trauma that Carolyn and Julian had endured. Their physical state bore testimony to the harrowing circumstances they had survived—

severe sunburns, an assortment of bug bites, and an array of cuts and bruises adorned their bodies. While the path to recovery was evident, the emotional scars were bound to run much deeper.

Guided by their priority to ensure the safety of Julian and Carolyn, the police entered their hospital room. Their initial interaction was marked by a delicate balance of relief and caution. Ensuring their well-being took precedence, but the urgency to gather information about the ordeal loomed large. The police acknowledged the gravity of their traumatic experiences and, while navigating with sensitivity, sought to piece together the events that had unfolded.

Acknowledging the potential gravity of their ordeal, the police stressed that any information about the identity of those responsible and the details of their experience would be of utmost significance. The looming presence of the ONA cult added an air of urgency to the investigation. Independently, Julian and Carolyn provided their testimonies to the police, offering insights that held the promise of unravelling the truth behind their disappearance and the unsettling occurrences that had unfolded. The convergence of these two narratives held the potential to provide a comprehensive understanding of a reality that had been veiled in secrecy —an understanding that was poised to reshape perceptions and challenge the limits of belief and understanding.

Here is the account that both Julian and Carolyn provided to the police:

Seven days earlier, Julian found himself outside the car, drawn back to the roadside where a lifeless animal lay. He reached down to clear away a branch obstructing his view, intending to examine the creature. Suddenly, a movement behind him caught him off guard. Before he could identify the source, a powerful blow struck the back of his head, rendering him unconscious.

Upon regaining consciousness, Julian instantly sensed the passage of considerable time. Daylight had given way to darkness, marking the hours that he had been unconscious. His disoriented gaze took in the unfamiliar forest surroundings. Stripped of his clothing, his wrists and ankles were bound to a tree directly behind him. Bewildered and uncertain, he surveyed his surroundings, but no answers presented themselves. A stroke of luck revealed a knife nestled among the leaves nearby. Puzzled by its presence, he seized the opportunity, he hastily cut himself loose and without a clear direction, fled into the night, fearing his abductor's return.

Simultaneously, as Julian grappled with his ordeal, Carolyn remained in the car, growing increasingly anxious for his safety. Stepping out onto the dirt road, she gazed down its winding path, her concern mounting. A chilling sight awaited her – a figure cloaked in black, wearing a balaclava, standing a mere ten feet away. Paralyzed with fear, she stood frozen as the figure charged at her. Overwhelmed, Carolyn was subdued, stripped of her clothing, and bound. Hogtied and blindfolded, she lay vulnerable on the road, left alone as her assailant departed.

Minutes later, the sound of an approaching car disrupted her despair. She was lifted from the ground and unceremoniously confined within its trunk. Hours passed in agonizing discomfort, the bindings constricting her limbs and cutting off circulation. Eventually, the car turned onto a rough terrain, its halt signaling an unknown destination. The driver's actions sent a surge of anxiety through her – the trunk opened, the blindfold lifted, and she found herself face to face with the man in the balaclava.

Thrown to the ground, she was dragged into the woods, her heart heavy with the dread of impending doom. The chilling reality of her situation bore down as she was deposited onto the forest floor. The man's ominous actions with a shovel amplified her terror; he purposefully showcased the tool as he began to dig a pit before her. She watched in horror, convinced he was digging her grave. Hours seemed to stretch as the pit grew deeper, the threat of death looming.

Finally, when the grave appeared complete, the man abandoned his task, discarding the shovel. Approaching her, he seized her and cast her into the pit. Desperation and fear gripped Carolyn as she knelt on the cold earth. As her assailant walked away, her prayers took form, her anxiety gradually eased by the fading sound of his footsteps. While her tormentor seemed to have departed, she remained trapped, exposed to the elements, her nakedness a stark reminder of her vulnerability.

After Julian successfully extricated himself from his bindings with the knife he had discovered, he wasted no time in fleeing and calling out for help. Though he was aware that his cries might alert their captor, the urgency of the situation and the biting cold compelled him to seek assistance immediately. With urgency in his voice, his shouts were met with an unexpected response – Carolyn's familiar voice. Despite the darkness shrouding the forest, Julian navigated through the trees toward the source of the sound. His persistence led him to Carolyn, confined in a hole, restrained and calling out for him.

In the hushed tones of fear and desperation, they shared their harrowing experiences. Julian recounted his assault, while Carolyn recounted the horrifying sequence that led her to the same grim location. With their apprehension of the assailant's potential return ever-present, Julian decided to descend into the hole. Armed with the knife, he swiftly severed Carolyn's restraints, facilitating her escape from the pit. Despite her body's protest, hampered by hours of restricted circulation, they resolved to leave the site behind.

Supported by Julian, Carolyn struggled to walk as they distanced themselves from the haunting hole. In their departure, their vigilance remained high, their eyes scanning the surroundings for any ominous traces. A mere stone's throw from the hole, their keen eyes uncovered a sleeping bag leaned against a tree, concealing vital sustenance. Inside, provisions of food and water were tightly bundled. Amidst their dire circumstances, the irony of their luck – both sinister and salvatory – struck them deeply.

Seizing the lifeline offered by the supplies, they grasped the sleeping bag, food, and water, and set off on a determined sprint. Over the subsequent two days, the sun's merciless heat punished them, leaving their skin blistered and scorched. Nights brought little reprieve, as plummeting temperatures drove them to huddle within their lone sleeping bag, rationing their meagre resources. Fueled by hope and a relentless will to survive, they pressed onward, convinced that each step would bring them closer to rescue. Yet, their optimism waned as the grueling hours and treacherous landscape seemed to stretch endlessly.

Tragically, at the end of those initial 48 hours, their sense of direction faltered, leading them back to the very site they had sought to escape. The hole yawned before them, a chilling reminder of their ordeal. Mercifully, no sign of their captor lingered. Though disheartened by their unintended circular path, the couple's inadvertent return held a silver lining. Propped against a tree, they found a backpack, brimming with provisions, clothing, and a map of their surroundings. Mystified by the serendipity of their discoveries, they hesitated but a moment before seizing the lifeline.

Aware that their assailant's return was likely imminent, they fled with newfound determination, carrying the backpack laden with hope. Their days continued to be marked by sunburns and chills, as they navigated the wilderness using the map as their guide. After five relentless days, their efforts led them to a road. Their bedraggled appearance caught the attention of a passing farmer, who promptly conveyed them to the hospital, where their remarkable tale of survival would finally be heard.

The police swiftly coordinated an extensive search throughout the expanse of Alpine National Park. Their focus was unwavering – the urgent need to locate the man in the balaclava who held potential connections to ONA or might be a lead to unravel the mystery. The vast sweep of the search yielded no sign of the balaclava-clad man or the elusive ONA. However, a significant discovery emerged at the location of the dug hole where Carolyn had been confined.

Thorough investigation of the area revealed crucial evidence – a shovel, rope, and duct tape. As these items underwent scrutiny, a shocking revelation emerged: they all belonged to Julian. This puzzling find presented two possible scenarios – either the kidnapper had appropriated Julian's supplies before committing the abduction, or, more ominously, Julian himself had been involved in the abduction in some capacity, providing the tools to the kidnapper. Faced with this perplexing evidence, the police approached Julian and directly confronted him, emphasizing the incongruity between his items and the crime.

At first, Julian vehemently rebuffed any suggestion of being involved in the kidnapping. He adamantly denied any culpability, asserting his innocence in the matter. Despite the weight of the accusations bearing down on him, Julian stood resolute in his denial. However, as the police interrogation intensified and the mounting pressure began to wear him down, Julian eventually cracked.

The truth behind the events of March 4th reveals a markedly different narrative. On the day Julian and Carolyn vanished, a meticulously planned scheme unfolded. As Julian picked up Carolyn, they headed down the dirt road leading to the forest and the waterfall. During their journey, Julian weaved a tale about spotting peculiar roadkill, claiming they had driven past it before Carolyn could see. However, this was a fabricated story intended to serve as a pretext for his subsequent actions. In reality, the roadkill he mentioned was a fiction, part of a calculated ruse to set in motion a series of events.

Their picnic at the waterfall completed, they embarked on their return journey. Feigning another interest in the non-existent roadkill, Julian requested to step out of the car. Concealing his true intent, he headed out of sight and retrieved his concealed gear—an all-black attire, the black balaclava, the knife, the shovel, the rope, and the duct tape. Out of view from Carolyn, Julian dressed himself and began retracing his steps, intent on executing his plan.

Reaching Carolyn, who had innocently awaited his return, Julian pounced suddenly, tackling her to the ground. He forcibly stripped her of her clothes, binding her in a hog-tie position, then thrust her into the car. With ruthless efficiency, he gathered his gear and supplies, seizing Carolyn's helplessness to further his designs. His intention was clear: a malevolent abduction had been set into motion.

Driving for hours northward, Julian's destination was Alpine National Park. There, he sought a remote forest trail. Parking the car off the beaten path, he opened the trunk, dragged Carolyn out, and cast her onto the ground. Propping her blindfolded form in front of the newly procured shovel, Julian heightened the terror by demonstrating his intent to bury her alive. He wanted to instill profound fear, an anguish that went beyond mere survival.

As Julian began to dig the hole, Carolyn, unable to see his actions, was left to confront the horrifying prospect of imminent death. With calculated precision, Julian completed the charade, positioning her as if for burial, before retreating out of sight. Having staged this theatrical display of menace, he discarded his clothes by a nearby tree and approached the scene anew, fully naked save for the knife he used as his apparent means of escape.

In a calculated ruse, Julian began yelling for help, directing his voice toward the pit where Carolyn was confined. She responded in kind, a desperate exchange that appeared to be a chance rescue. Upon reaching her, Julian spun an intricate web of lies, weaving a story of his own captivity and escape. He positioned himself as the valiant savior, attempting to alleviate her distress and gain her trust.

With Carolyn liberated from the pit, Julian led her away from the scene, towing the sleeping bag and supplies he had left behind earlier. Their escape into the wilderness was his calculated maneuver, executed with precision and purpose. Over the ensuing days, as they braved harsh conditions, Julian maintained a deliberate path, knowledgeable of their surroundings. The accidental return to the site of the pit, as well as the "discovery" of a second set of supplies, were all facets of his elaborate strategy.

Upon confronting Julian with the compelling evidence of his actions, his confession painted a disturbing picture. His motives, it appeared, were driven by a deeply misguided pursuit. Julian revealed that his actions were rooted in an agonizing impatience. Both he and Carolyn were devoutly committed to their religious beliefs, including abstaining from premarital intercourse. As their wedding remained a year away, Julian's desire overpowered him, prompting him to orchestrate this elaborate charade in the hopes of coercing Carolyn into breaking their vow of chastity.

During their seven-day ordeal in Alpine National Park, Julian and Carolyn faced their dire circumstances with minimal or no clothing, relying on one sleeping bag Julian had strategically placed beforehand. Aware of their vulnerability to the harsh elements, Julian manipulated their intimate closeness as a pretense to persuade Carolyn to have sex for survival. Under the pretext of generating enough warmth to fend off the cold, he pressed her repeatedly, asserting that it was a matter of life or death. However, Carolyn steadfastly refused, standing firm in her convictions despite their dire predicament.

As the days unfolded, Julian's attempts to sway Carolyn proved futile. Her resolute "no" remained unwavering, even when confronted with the extremity of their situation. In the end, Julian's persistence gave way to resignation, and the ordeal concluded without him achieving his goal.

In a startling revelation to the police, Julian confessed to being the author of the notes that preceded the kidnapping. He admitted that he had fabricated the connection to the Order of the Nine Angles, hoping it would shift suspicion away from him and create a diversion prior to his eventual trial.

Before facing trial for his kidnapping charges, Julian was granted bail. Seizing this opportunity, he decided to evade Australian authorities by altering his appearance. He darkened his skin and hair, adopting a fake Indian passport in an attempt to escape to India. While he managed to deceive Australian officials temporarily, his ruse was exposed upon arrival in India. Swiftly identified, he was repatriated to Australia, where he would stand trial for his actions.

In 2009, Julian faced the consequences of his actions when he was pronounced guilty of kidnapping, along with a string of related charges. The court sentenced him to seven years and nine months in prison, marking the culmination of a disturbing chapter that had unfolded with chilling intricacy.

"SHATTERED INNOCENCE: UNMASKING THE DARKNESS BEHIND JESSIE BLODGETT'S TRAGIC END"

Snuggled within a quiet town in the heart of America lies a two-story house. It exudes an unassuming aura, its simplicity and plainness making it blend seamlessly with its surroundings. Cloaked behind a curtain of trees, it remains hidden from the casual passerby on the road, revealing only glimpses of its presence. Yet, the events that unfolded within its walls have forever altered the perception of this unremarkable abode.

Nestled in the heart of America lies Hartford, Wisconsin. The town boasts downtown's grandest automobile museum in all of Wisconsin, while a nearby bowling alley, Dave's Lanes, entices with its budget-friendly beer and pizza. Just around the corner, local favorites like Scoop Deville, a 1950s-themed ice cream parlor renowned for raspberry sundaes, and The Mine Shaft, a spacious family-friendly restaurant offering comfort food and arcade games, beckon visitors. Hartford's verdant Woodlawn and Willowbrook parks offer pristine walking trails, and the bustling Shower Arts Centre stages local theatre performances, making it a popular gathering spot. Yet, these attractions pale in comparison to the town's most unforgettable story—the tragedy of Jessie Blodgett.

Jessie Blodgett's life was undoubtedly extraordinary. Born in 1994 to her loving parents, Buck and Joy Blodgett, her arrival brought immeasurable joy after years of their longing. The Blodgett's had faced infertility struggles for a long time, making Jessie's birth a truly cherished moment, attended by Buck's mother and a midwife, and holding special significance as a treasured home event.

Subsequently, the family relocated from Atlanta, Georgia, to Hartford, Wisconsin, where Jessie's formative years were spent in their modest two-story home, conveniently situated a short drive from downtown.

Within this unassuming home, Jessie's talents shone brightly, as she was a gifted musician who played the piano, violin, and possessed a captivating singing voice. Not only was she admired for her musical prowess, but also for her unwavering commitment to justice; early on, Jessie developed a strong moral compass and championed causes such as animal rights, environmental issues, social justice, and ending violence against women. By the time she graduated from high school in 2012, Jessie was a revered figure among her peers, teachers, and parents alike, known for her wisdom beyond her years.

Jessie's determination to change the world led her to pursue a career in music education. Enrolling at the University of Wisconsin in Milwaukee, she excelled in the musical education program, even earning a talent scholarship for her outstanding performance. Returning to Hartford during the summer breaks, Jessie immersed herself in her burgeoning career, teaching voice, piano, and violin to local children. She also pursued her passion for music, collaborating with friend Dan Bartelt and participating in local musicals, including a leading role in "Fiddler on the Roof."

During one summer, after a successful opening weekend of "Fiddler on the Roof," Jessie attended a pool party with fellow cast members. Later that night, she returned home, visibly perturbed by advances from older members of the cast. While she initially dismissed it as discomfort, her demeanor spoke otherwise. The next morning, her parents went about their routines, unaware that something sinister had unfolded.

Joy Blodgett, Jessie's mother, returned home around noon to find her daughter's absence alarming. Expecting Jessie to be awake and attending to her student's lesson, Joy knocked on her daughter's door but received no response. Entering the room, she found Jessie still asleep and left her laundry before proceeding with her day. Hours later, Joy returned, only to discover that Jessie had not surfaced. Alarmed and perplexed, she ventured upstairs to wake her daughter, but what she found stopped her in her tracks. Her frantic call to 911 marked the beginning of a devastating mystery that would forever alter Hartford's peaceful facade. Here is the 911 Audio Transcription - Joy's Call:

Joy: "Oh my God, oh my God!" Dispatcher: "Hartford 911, what's your emergency?" Joy: "My daughter is blue. I went to wake her up, and I just got home from lunch, and she won't wake up. Oh my God!" Dispatcher: "Hang on, 2 seconds." Joy: "Okay." Dispatcher: "Okay, so she... is she breathing?" Joy: "I don't think so, no! Her pants are all wet, and she's got... it looks like strangulation marks." Dispatcher: "There are strangulation marks?" Joy: "That's what it looks like. I don't know what's going on. I don't know what's going on."

Joy gently pulled her daughter out of the bed and laid her down on the ground. She placed a pillow underneath Jessie's head and then began doing chest compressions in a desperate attempt to save her daughter's life. However, it was already too late. When police and paramedics arrived moments later, they entered the bedroom and quickly determined that Jessie was deceased. The marks on her neck that her mother had mentioned during the 911 call were indeed present, along with similar marks on her left wrist and ankles. These findings led the on-scene police to conclude that this was not a natural death, suicide, or accident. This was a homicide.

With great care, the police guided Joy out of her daughter's bedroom and directed her downstairs. The bedroom had become a crime scene, and preserving its integrity was essential for gathering evidence to solve the case. Downstairs, Joy was reunited with her deeply distressed husband, Buck. Their world had been shattered in an instant—their beloved daughter, their only child, was suddenly gone, and it defied all understanding.

During the search of Jessie's bedroom and the Blodgett house, the police found no cords, ropes, or ligatures that could have been used for strangulation. Moreover, there were no signs of forced entry anywhere in the house, and nothing appeared to be stolen. With these puzzling circumstances,

Hartford's lead detective, Richard Thickens, began operating under the assumption that the perpetrator was familiar with Jessie, had knowledge of her whereabouts in the house, and knew how to enter. It seemed they targeted her specifically and then left after committing the crime.

In discussions with Buck and Joy shortly after they discovered their daughter's lifeless body, Detective Thickens asked if they had any ideas about who could have wanted to harm Jessie. At first, the parents claimed ignorance, not suspecting anyone. However, with further questioning, Buck mentioned recent tree limb cutters who had worked near Jessie's bedroom window, speculating that they might have seen a vulnerable teenage girl alone in her room and decided to attack. Additionally, Jessie had recently been working at a local restaurant and had clashed with a co-worker who invaded her personal space. This co-worker could have been seeking revenge, as they were aware of Jessie's distress and had caused her family concern. Furthermore, Joy noted that Jessie had appeared upset the previous night, mentioning two older guys who made her uncomfortable at a party.

Though they hadn't delved into the issue, it was clear something had been bothering Jessie.

Detective Thickens pursued leads, investigating the tree trimmers and the co-worker. Both had solid alibis and were ruled out as suspects. The two older guys from the party were also investigated, resulting in one being cleared of suspicion, while the other, Randy Talley, remained uncertain. When interviewed, Randy denied any involvement in Jessie's death. He claimed he had been at his apartment since after the party and had no one to corroborate his whereabouts.

The police continued their search of Jessie's room and found her diary, which contained an entry that intensified suspicions about Randy. Despite downplaying the incident with the older cast members at the pool party to her mother, Jessie's final diary entry indicated otherwise. She expressed strong upset over their actions, stating that they were corrupting her and turning innocent affection into a competition. Her closing lines hinted at an expected confrontation with these individuals. The entry raised questions about

Randy's potential involvement.

However, Randy's lack of an alibi and Jessie's ominous diary entry were not sufficient to definitively link him to the murder. His cell phone records indicated no interactions with Jessie leading up to her death. Additionally, his phone was in his apartment around the time of the murder, making it difficult to place him at the scene. While not conclusive proof of his innocence, this lack of evidence led the police to revisit their investigation, searching for new leads to pursue. Just 24 hours after Jessie's discovery, a significant breakthrough would provide them with a new direction.

Three days prior to Jessie's tragic death, a young woman named Melissa Richards decided to take her dog for a walk in a park located in Richfield, Wisconsin—a small town about 10 miles southeast of Hartford. As Melissa pulled her car into the dirt parking lot adjacent to the walking trail, she noticed only one other vehicle parked there. A blue minivan was positioned on her left, facing away from the entrance, with the driver's legs protruding out of the window. While this sight didn't particularly concern

Melissa, she still registered the presence of the person in the van.

Driving past the blue minivan, Melissa parked her own car on the opposite side of the dirt lot. She stepped out of the vehicle with her dog, Remy, and headed onto the walking trail that led into the woods. The trail formed a loop that would eventually bring her back to the entrance of the parking lot, meaning she would pass by the blue minivan again if it were still there. As she finished her 30-minute walk, Melissa reached the parking lot's entrance. The blue minivan remained in its spot, but now the driver was sitting in the passenger seat with the door open. While Melissa noticed this change, it didn't raise immediate concern, so she continued with her actions.

Releasing Remy's leash, Melissa observed her dog running towards the car. She unlocked the trunk with her key fob, allowing Remy to jump into the vehicle. As Remy leaped into the car, Melissa turned her attention back toward the blue minivan. However, the person who had previously been sitting in the driver's seat had now exited the vehicle and was standing there, staring intently at Melissa. Melissa acknowledged the person briefly, feeling somewhat startled, before quickly looking away and proceeding toward her car. She didn't want to appear impolite and chose to move forward without much concern.

As she walked a short distance beyond the blue minivan, Melissa heard footsteps rapidly approaching from behind. She swiftly turned around to find the same person who had been in the minivan now running towards her. Just as before, this individual abruptly stopped upon Melissa's gaze, leaving them standing about 10 feet apart. Melissa reflexively remarked, "Oh, you scared me," before shifting her focus away and resuming her path towards her vehicle. However, this time, an unsettling feeling crept in, suggesting that something was amiss. Glancing back at the person, Melissa noticed the knife they held in their right hand by their hip.

In a sudden and shocking turn of events, the person charged at Melissa, lunging forward to tackle her to the ground. She landed on her stomach, trapped beneath the weight of her assailant. Despite her vulnerable position, Melissa's determination didn't waver as she fought back with all her strength. Rolling over, she managed to grasp the blade of the knife and wrest it away from her attacker, pulling it beneath her body and securing it. Taken aback by Melissa's tenacity, the attacker hesitated before attempting to retrieve the knife from beneath her. Melissa refused to let go, prompting the attacker to sit back on her, asking if they could leave. Melissa declined, prompting the attacker to suddenly leap up and sprint back towards the blue minivan.

Understanding the danger, Melissa wasted no time. She hurriedly got up, still gripping the knife, and headed to her car. Tossing the bloodied knife onto the passenger seat floorboard, she ensured Remy was inside before locking the doors and placing the bloody weapon in her car. As she looked up, she saw her assailant hastily driving away in the blue minivan. Relieved yet shaken, Melissa started her car and drove straight to the hospital. Following 15 stitches to mend the deep cuts on her hands, she found herself in a recovery room where she met Joel Clausing, a detective with the

Washington County Sheriff's Department.

Melissa provided her statement to Detective Clausing, recounting the terrifying attack she had just experienced. Despite her shaken state, Melissa had an exceptional memory of the incident. She vividly described her attacker's appearance and even detailed the blue minivan they had driven. Melissa believed the vehicle was a Dodge Caravan minivan, likely dating from the years 2000 to 2002. With this detailed information, Detective Clausing compiled a composite sketch of the assailant and vehicle details, releasing the information to the media and throughout the community.

One day after Jessie's tragic death, on July 16th, a deputy from the Washington County Sheriff's Department came forward. He had seen the flyer with the description provided by Melissa Richards regarding the type of vehicle involved in the attack. He recognized the vehicle from his own experience, having seen it parked in the same spot at the park a couple of weeks earlier.

Something had struck him as odd back then—the driver's behavior was strange. Intrigued, he ran the license plates to check for any outstanding warrants, but the search yielded no results. While he had initially dismissed it, the description in the flyer now convinced him that it was the same vehicle. He decided to pull up the plates he had run and see if they matched.

However, upon examining the information from the license plates, Detective Clausing and the deputy discovered that the vehicle's owner did not match the detailed description provided by Melissa. Initially, they were inclined to dismiss it as a mere coincidence that a similar blue minivan had been parked in the same spot a few weeks apart. Yet, Detective Clausing delved deeper into the owner's connections and found a relative whose description aligned precisely with Melissa's attacker.

On the afternoon of July 16th, Detective Clausing used the phone number of this relative to contact them. As he placed the call, a vigil was being held in memory of Jessie Blodgett at her home. Close friends and family gathered in the living room, sharing their memories and mourning her loss. Amidst this emotional gathering, a phone began to ring within the circle. The owner of the phone, 19-year-old Daniel Bartelt, a close friend of Jessie's who had spent the summer creating music with her, stood up and moved away from the group to answer the call. Detective Clausing requested Daniel to come to the police station for an interview regarding Melissa Richards.

At the same time, 10 miles northwest, Jessie's parents, Buck and Joy Blodgett, were hosting a vigil in their home. Unbeknownst to them, Daniel was being brought into the station for questioning regarding an attack on another young woman, Melissa. The timing was eerie given Daniel's presence at a murder victim's home and his connection to another recent attack.

During the interview, Detective Clausing began by asking Daniel about his presence at Jessie's home. Daniel explained that he was a close friend of Jessie's and had attended the vigil in her memory since she had been tragically killed the day before. The detectives then shifted the conversation towards Melissa Richards, an attack Daniel vehemently denied any involvement in. However, they noticed cuts on Daniel's hands, leading them to inquire about their origin. Daniel initially claimed he had injured his hands while cooking, but under further scrutiny, he confessed to hurting himself while attacking Melissa Richards.

As the conversation unfolded, Detective Clausing probed deeper into Daniel's life. Daniel confessed that he had been unemployed for a while and had been pretending to go to work to avoid admitting the loss of his job to his parents. When asked about the motive behind attacking Melissa, Daniel admitted to feeling overwhelmed after dropping out of college and losing his job. He explained that he had attacked her to make someone else feel the same fear he was experiencing.

While Daniel confessed to attacking Melissa, he vehemently denied any involvement in Jessie Blodgett's murder. He professed his love for Jessie and insisted he would never harm her. However, Detective Clausing and his colleague couldn't overlook the unusual circumstances—Daniel being linked to two attacks on young women within days of each other.

Recognizing the implications, the detectives shared their concerns with the Hartford Police. They suggested looking into Daniel as a potential suspect in Jessie's murder, which raised the possibility that his lies extended even further. The unfolding revelations pointed to a much darker truth than initially apparent.

Daniel, despite his upbringing in a loving and supportive family, displayed signs of a disturbing transformation that left those who knew him baffled. He had been a brilliant student, maintaining straight A's, and he possessed remarkable musical talents that earned him respect from peers, teachers, and mentors alike. However, something had gone terribly awry within Daniel.

In the time leading up to his attack on Melissa, it became evident that Daniel's interests had taken a macabre turn. His internet search history painted a chilling picture: he had become fixated on themes of death, murder, and killing. Disturbingly, he spent extensive periods scouring the internet for actual snuff videos—gruesome recordings of real-life murders. He delved into research on serial killers and spree killers, exhibiting a particular fascination with those who targeted multiple women.

In the days immediately preceding his assault on Melissa, Daniel's search history took an even darker turn. He stumbled upon a particularly heinous pornographic snuff film featuring the brutal assault and strangulation of a restrained woman. Consumed by this disturbing content, Daniel viewed the video repeatedly, internalizing its graphic violence.

On that fateful day, July 12th, while feigning his presence at work, Daniel lingered in his car. As he observed Melissa alone, a disturbing connection was triggered in his mind. He resolved to replicate the vile acts depicted in the snuff film with Melissa as his victim. Positioned within the secluded confines of the dirt parking lot, Daniel's intentions were ominous. The tape discovered at the scene suggested he planned to immobilize and abduct Melissa, seeking to enact his violent fantasies.

However, Melissa's bravery and tenacity thwarted Daniel's plans. She fought back vigorously, causing him to panic and flee the scene. This initial failed attempt did not quench his disturbing desires, though. Just three days later, on July 15th, Daniel seemingly resolved to reattempt his horrific act, this time targeting Jessie.

The tragic irony lies in the sinister choice of Jessie as his victim. Being a close friend, she inherently placed her trust in Daniel and wouldn't have harbored suspicions about his presence. This trust likely facilitated his access to her home and, ultimately, her bedroom, where he committed the atrocious act that ended her life. Jessie's innocence and vulnerability, combined with her misplaced trust in her attacker, formed a perfect storm of tragedy. According to the account of an eyewitness who was driving through the Blodgett neighborhood on the morning of Jessie's murder, it is believed that Daniel arrived at the Blodgett household shortly after Buck and Joy had left for work. Pulling into the driveway, he was aware that Jessie was home alone. The exact details of their interaction inside the house remain uncertain—whether Jessie came downstairs to answer the door or if she was still upstairs sleeping. Nevertheless, Daniel entered the residence with a sinister purpose, carrying a bag containing a selection of supplies carefully chosen for his grim intent.

His bag held a disturbing assortment of items: specialized tape, ligatures, cords, ropes, alcohol wipes, and zip ties. Armed with these tools, he ascended the stairs to Jessie's bedroom. Whether she was awake or asleep at the time remains a haunting question. Daniel wasted no time; he pounced on her, swiftly inserting a homemade ball gag into her mouth and securing it with the special tape. Deprived of her ability to vocalize, he bound her wrists and ankles, subjecting her to a hog-tie restraint.

What followed was a horrifying act of violence. Daniel viciously assaulted Jessie before ultimately strangling her with a cord. Once her life had been extinguished, he attempted to erase traces of his crime by cleaning her body with alcohol wipes. He then meticulously rearranged her in her bed, positioning the covers over her to create the illusion that she was still peacefully asleep—a cruel facade for her unsuspecting parents who would later discover her lifeless form.

After collecting his macabre tools back into his bag, Daniel inadvertently left behind one of the rolls of the specialized tape beneath Jessie's bed. He slipped out of the Blodgett home and made his way to Woodlawn Park, where he disposed of his chilling supplies in a trash can.

The day after Jessie's tragic death, a vigil was held in her memory. Incredibly, Daniel attended the vigil, where he exhibited a stark contrast in behavior. According to those in attendance, he was unusually talkative and engaged in conversation—a striking and disturbing contrast to the heinous acts he had perpetrated just a day earlier.

Daniel would ultimately be convicted of the murder of Jessie Blodgett, though he never admitted his guilt. Buck Blodgett, Jessie's grieving father, delivered a poignant and heartrending speech that captured the profound loss he felt as a parent who had lost his only child. Addressing the judge, he turned to face Daniel, locking eyes with him, and uttered words of forgiveness and compassion. "Dan, I forgive you, as I have every day since I found out it was you," Buck proclaimed. And in a moment of astonishing grace, he added, "Not only do I forgive you, but I love you."

When Daniel was given the opportunity to speak in his own defense, he looked directly at Buck and Joy, Jessie's parents. He maintained his innocence, asserting that he had no answers to provide because he was not responsible for Jessie's death. His conscience, he claimed, was clear. Despite the overwhelming evidence against him, he clung to his denial. As a result of the trial's outcome, Daniel was sentenced to life in prison without the possibility of parole.

In the aftermath of Jessie's tragic passing, Buck Blodgett, driven by the desire to honor his daughter's memory and effect positive change, took an amazing step. Instead of succumbing to the weight of his grief, he channeled his emotions into a purposeful endeavor. He initiated the Love Is Greater Than Hate Project, a remarkable charitable organization with a powerful mission to combat male-on-female violence. This initiative aimed to turn the tragedy of Jessie's death into a catalyst for positive change, echoing the aspirations that Jessie herself had expressed—to make a difference and reshape the world for the better.

"SECRETS OF THE SILENT HIGHWAY: THE PUZZLING DISAPPEARANCE OF DEVIN WILLIAMS"

One morning in 1995, nestled within their modest nylon tent deep within a vast Arizona forest, two campers found themselves immersed in the serenity of nature. However, their tranquility was abruptly shattered by an unexpected disturbance. A resounding rumbling sound began to echo through the air, capturing their attention and curiosity.

Intrigued, they cautiously unzipped their tent flap and turned their gaze toward the source of the noise. Their eyes fixed on a dirt road that stretched ahead, where an enormous cloud of dust and dirt was rapidly advancing towards them. As the cloud neared, a distinct shape materialized within its heart, revealing an object that immediately struck both campers as profoundly out of place within the confines of this forest.

In a matter of seconds, the object surged past them, disappearing into the dense canopy of trees in the opposite direction. Left momentarily dumbfounded, the campers grappled with the bewildering sight before them. Attempting to rationalize the presence of such an anomalous entity, they exchanged thoughts and hypotheses, only to be interrupted once again by the resumption of the rumbling sound.

Their gazes snapped back to the dirt road, and true to their expectation, the colossal presence was returning, the rumbling growing louder as it approached once more.

Late in the night of May 27, 1995, Devin Williams, a long-haul truck driver, parked his refrigerated semi-truck at a truck stop in Kingman, Arizona. Exhausted and growing increasingly frustrated, he rolled out his sleeping bag in the sleeper cab of his truck. Typically, Devin would use this time to catch some sleep during the night, but sleep evaded him on this occasion. Having been on the road for days, his eagerness to complete his route and reunite with his wife Mary Lou and their three children in Americus, Kansas, only intensified.

Devin's primary concern was his family. Despite his tough exterior and his rugged trucker appearance, he was a devoted family man. He hated being away from his loved ones for extended periods, a necessity of his job as a long-haul driver. The financial pressure of a new home purchase added to his stress, compelling him to keep driving even when sleep was hard to come by.

As the night wore on, Devin's frustration grew, impacting his sleep further. He decided to abandon the attempt and left the sleeper cab to head into the truck stop. He made a call to his boss, Tom Wilson, explaining his inability to sleep and assuring him that he would still reach Kansas City on time for the delivery. Devin was known for his reliability, and Tom had no reason to doubt him.

The following Monday morning,

however, the distribution center in Kansas City contacted Tom, reporting that Devin had not arrived as scheduled. Tom initially dismissed their concern, assuming Devin would show up shortly. Yet, when more time passed without any sign of Devin, Tom grew worried. He contacted other drivers, hoping for information about Devin's whereabouts, but no one had heard from him.

Tom's worry escalated when he received a call from Devin's wife, Mary Lou, inquiring about her missing husband. As Tom explained the situation, Mary Lou became increasingly alarmed. She contacted the police, initiating a missing person report. Law enforcement agencies along Devin's potential route were alerted to look for any signs of him.

Following the issuance of the alert, the officer received a prompt callback from the Coconino County Sheriff's Department in Arizona. Coconino County was situated 200 miles to the east of Kingman, Arizona, where Devin had struggled to sleep on that Saturday night. Curiously, the Coconino County Sheriff's Department informed the police officer in America's Kansas that they had no information regarding Devin's whereabouts. However, they were well aware of the location of his truck.

Strangely, practically everyone in Coconino County was familiar with Devin's truck. It had become a topic of conversation and attention throughout the county.

On the preceding Sunday, just a day before Devin was reported missing, someone driving his truck embarked on a day of unsettling behavior, causing distress among hikers and campers within the vast Tonto National Forest in Coconino County, Arizona. The Tonto National Forest, a sprawling wilderness preserve spanning 600,000 acres, was significantly distant from Devin's usual trucking route — a location that seemed entirely incongruous for a massive semi-truck weighing 10 tons and stretching 48 feet in length. Located around 20 miles off the highway, the narrow forest roads could hardly accommodate small vehicles, let alone such an enormous truck.

On that early Sunday morning,

approximately eight hours after Devin had spoken with his boss Tom, a pair of hikers named Lynn and Jack Yarrington found themselves inside their tent in the heart of the Tonto National Forest. Their campsite was located near a dirt road. Suddenly, the distant sound of rumbling reached their ears. Curiosity piqued, they unzipped their tent and gazed toward the road. Initially, all they perceived was a cloud of dust and smoke billowing forth. Soon, within the haze emerged Devin's colossal truck, hurtling down the road at near-full speed. The massive vehicle sped past them, vanishing in the opposite direction. Baffled but not alarmed, Jack and Lynn conjectured that perhaps the driver had lost their way and was attempting to turn around.

Their theory was seemingly confirmed when, moments later, they heard the sound of the truck's engine approaching again. This time, Devin's truck returned from the opposite direction. Observing this bizarre behavior, the couple concluded that the driver must have managed to reverse direction after realizing they were off course. Engaged in light-hearted banter about the situation, they suddenly heard the familiar rumbling once more. Gazing up, they witnessed the truck charging back down the road. This time, they noted something unusual — a small sedan was also on the road, headed toward a collision with the oncoming truck.

Reacting swiftly, Jack and Lynn shouted and waved their arms frantically at the truck, urging the driver to slow down. Regrettably, the truck maintained its breakneck speed, showing no signs of deceleration. Meanwhile, the sedan driver, alerted by the couple's actions, halted the car, assessing the situation. The sedan's driver quickly realized the impending danger and maneuvered the car off the road to avoid the impending collision. Miraculously, the truck narrowly missed the sedan and continued unabated, appearing as though the driver was oblivious to the close call.

The sedan's driver, visibly shaken by the near-miss, informed Jack and Lynn that he had locked eyes with the truck's driver during the encounter. He described the truck's operator as unresponsive and expressionless, gripping the wheel with unwavering focus as if disregarding the sedan entirely.

Later that same day, a separate incident occurred nearby within Tonto National Forest. A family was enjoying a hiking trip when they stumbled upon a peculiar scene — Devin's truck inexplicably positioned in the middle of a vast open field. Perplexed, the family observed a man standing beside the truck, gazing into the distance. Concerned that the driver might be stranded, the family's father approached to offer assistance. However, as he neared, he noticed something disconcerting about the man's demeanor.

Rather than engaging in conversation, the man continued to stare vacantly ahead, his mouth slowly widening without speech. His lower jaw began to oscillate rapidly, producing a rapid clicking sound as if in the throes of an involuntary action. Alarmed, the family's father retreated, feeling an eerie sense that something was amiss. When the man finally acknowledged the father's presence, he delivered a cryptic message: "I didn't do it, they did it." This unnerving encounter prompted the family to report the incident to the police, sharing their disconcerting experience with the truck's driver.

It would take a Coconino County Sheriff's Department deputy some time to navigate the route to the Meadow where the truck and the unidentified man were last seen. Upon arriving, the deputy confirmed the truck's presence, exactly as described by the concerned father. However, the truck was deserted, with no one in sight. The engine was still running, and upon inspecting the cab, the deputy found everything orderly and neat. He also discovered the truck's cargo — a substantial load of strawberries and lettuce — intact in the refrigerated back section. Perplexed, the deputy checked the truck's license plate against the database, but no records matched the situation. At that point, he arranged for a towing company to recover the truck from the Meadow.

Over the subsequent 24 hours, Devin's disappearance was reported, prompting Coconino County Sheriff's Department to coordinate with law enforcement in Americus, Kansas. The department confirmed the discovery of Devin's truck but had no further information to provide. The inexplicable behavior exhibited by the man driving the truck through the Tonto National Forest stood in stark contrast to Devin's character and history. Witnesses, including Lynn and Jack Yarrington, who witnessed the truck's erratic driving, insisted that the man they saw driving matched Devin's appearance. Nevertheless, there was no logical explanation for Devin to venture into the Tonto National Forest with his massive truck, which was ill-suited for the forest's narrow dirt roads.

Devin's motivations seemed clear — his sole desire was to reunite with his wife and children in Americus, Kansas. Financially, while not overly affluent, their situation was stable and improving as they worked to renovate their new home. Devin's strong relationship with his wife and lack of any known problems in his personal life further contradicted the possibility of him running away. Likewise, kidnapping was deemed unlikely due to Devin's imposing presence as a tattooed, cowboy-hat-wearing truck driver.

Devin's medical and psychological well-being also eliminated several potential theories. He had no history of medical issues, mental health struggles, neurological abnormalities, or drug use. In fact, he consistently passed drug tests as part of his job requirements.

An intriguing development emerged when Jack and Lynn Yarrington, who had witnessed Devin's truck maneuvers and near-collision, shared their account with searchers. They claimed to have spotted Devin on foot, barefoot, and irrationally aggressive a day before his disappearance was reported. As they encountered this individual. Instead of a calm response, he reacted by hurling a rock at their car. This peculiar and unprovoked act left them deeply perplexed and disturbed.

With no breakthrough and nearly three weeks of searching, authorities reluctantly called off the search for Devin, leaving his disappearance shrouded in mystery. The bizarre circumstances surrounding his truck's presence in the forest, the unknown man driving it, and Devin's subsequent vanishing, confounded investigators and left a trail of unanswered questions.

Then, on May 2nd, 1997, nearly two years after Devin had been reported missing, a significant development unfolded. Two hikers were trekking along a trail within the heart of Tonto National Forest, precisely the area where exhaustive searches for Devin had taken place two years earlier. Ahead of them lay an incongruous sight: a white object positioned directly on the trail. Intrigued, they approached and discovered that the object was, in fact, a complete human skull – devoid of its accompanying skeleton. Astonished, the hikers were confronted with the reality of encountering an actual human head. Puzzled by the mystery surrounding its presence and why they seemed to be the first to stumble upon it, they promptly contacted the authorities. Responding officers collected the skull, subjecting it to DNA analysis which ultimately confirmed its identity as belonging to Devin Williams.

While the discovery of Devin's skull provides a tangible link to his enigmatic story, no conclusive explanation has emerged to elucidate the events that transpired. A plethora of theories have been proposed, ranging from the possibility of a sudden medical ailment precipitating his inexplicable behavior, to speculative suggestions of drug use despite his clean history. In the realm of the paranormal, some even entertain notions that extraterrestrial intervention might account for his strange conduct, culminating in an alien abduction that inexplicably led to his skull's reappearance on the forest trail. Yet, despite these diverse conjectures, the mystery of Devin's fate remains unsolved, rendering each theory as plausible or improbable as the next.

"THE DARK WATERS OF TRAGEDY: THE ROGERS FAMILY'S HORRIFYING FATE"

Situated on the far western side of Ohio lies the tranquil town of Wilshire. In the year 1989, this close-knit community was home to fewer than 600 residents, mostly comprising middle-class Americans. Many were engaged in farming, factory work, or contributed to the handful of small local businesses. While Wilshire might not have been the most exhilarating place to reside, it boasted a reputation as an idyllic environment for raising families.

Among the families embedded in the Wilshire community was the Rogers family. The parents, Hal and Joan, the latter often referred to as Joe, were both

36 years old at the time. Their household also included their two daughters, 17-year-old Michelle and 14-year-old Christy.

Hal and Joe's love story had its roots in high school, where their personalities couldn't have been more contrasting. Joe was outgoing and enjoyed popularity, while Hal was reserved and understated. Despite these differences, they formed a harmonious partnership that seemed to bring out the best in each other. During their senior year, Joe became pregnant with Michelle, prompting the teenage couple to tie the knot after graduation. They embarked on their life journey by settling on a dairy farm.

In the years that followed, Hal and Joe dedicated themselves wholeheartedly to their farm. However, their efforts proved insufficient to cover their expenses. To make ends meet, Joe took on a night job at a factory, operating a forklift and contributing to the assembly line. While life was marked by its challenges for the Rogers family, they maintained an unwavering positive outlook. The daughters thrived in school, forming friendships with ease, and relished their time at home engaging with the cherished farm animals.

Despite their busy lives, Hal and Joe always found moments to steal away for a quiet meal, nurturing their connection. However, their serene and joyful way of life would be shattered later that year when a devastating truth emerged: Hal's brother, John, who resided in a trailer on their farm property, had been secretly assaulting Michelle. For three long years, Michelle refrained from confiding in anyone due to John's menacing threats, which included the promise to end her life. The revelation took a new and horrifying turn when inappropriate pictures of Michelle were discovered within John's trailer. His sinister secret was laid bare, resulting in his incarceration for a long time. Nonetheless, the damage he left in his wake was beyond measure. Michelle was left traumatized to the extent that discussing her ordeal was nearly impossible.

Meanwhile, Hal, her father, was overwhelmed with shock. The realization that his own brother had inflicted harm upon his daughter, right under his nose, was almost unbearable. The idea of vengeance crossed his mind, but John's custody prevented any direct action. Adding to the heartache, their mother sided with John, accusing Michelle of fabricating the ordeal. This belief spread through the town, compounding the tragedy.

Amidst this turmoil, Hal and Joe contemplated a potential solution: a vacation. A getaway from the farm, the drama, and the stress. A chance for the girls to simply be kids again, if only for a few days. Hal, opting to remain behind, decided that Joe and the girls should embark on a mother-daughter trip. The girls, upon hearing the news, were elated, having never experienced a vacation before. They were tasked with planning the trip, bearing in mind the budget and the fact that they would be driving to their destination. After careful consideration, they settled on Florida.

For weeks, they meticulously crafted their itinerary, aiming to make the most of their journey and the destination. On May 26, 1989, they bid farewell to Hal and set off in the light blue family sedan. Driving for approximately eight hours on I-75, they crossed Ohio, Kentucky, and Tennessee, arriving in Georgia as their midway point. After resting at a motel, they resumed their journey, reaching Florida the following morning. Over the next few days, they adhered to their planned itinerary, exploring amusement parks, zoos, and various attractions throughout the state.

On June 1st, the trio left Orlando and headed to Tampa for another day of enjoyment. They intended to return to Ohio on June 3rd, but when that day came and went without their arrival, Hal remained calm. However, as more days passed with no communication, concern began to settle in. Finally, on June 6th, Hal reported his family missing to the police. Despite initial assumptions that they were simply prolonging their vacation, the situation changed dramatically just two days later.

On that morning in Tampa, Florida, a motel maid noticed something peculiar about room 251. Having cleaned the room just a week before, she was baffled to find it exactly as she had left it—beds neatly made, towels untouched, and luggage undisturbed. Intrigued by this oddity, she informed her manager, who promptly alerted the police about the situation.

Responding to the call, Tampa police discovered that the registered occupants of room 251 were Joan Rogers and her two daughters, Michelle and Christy—individuals who were reported missing. The trio had checked into the motel on June 1st, but thereafter, they had seemingly vanished without a trace. A search of their room revealed little substantial evidence, apart from their camera containing two final pictures: one depicting Michelle preparing to head out, and the other capturing the sun setting over Tampa Bay from their room's balcony.

As the investigation unfolded, the authorities located Joan's car about a mile from the motel, parked near a public boat ramp. Yet, neither Joan nor her daughters were present. The discovery of two brochures inside the car raised even more questions. One brochure held handwritten directions to the boat ramp, penned by Joan herself. The other note, however, bore a handwriting unfamiliar to the family.

The focus initially centered on Joan's directions, specifically the concluding words: "blue with white." Investigators deduced that these words were meant to steer her towards identifying something blue and white upon reaching the boat ramp. This logical deduction naturally led them to consider boats.

Tragically, the police made a grim connection. Four days prior, the Coast Guard had made a distressing find in the bay—approximately 25 miles from the location of Joan's abandoned car. At the time, no one had connected this discovery to the three missing women from Ohio. Yet, with the newfound awareness of their disappearance, the correlation became starkly evident.

Although it would take three years to piece together the puzzle, the authorities eventually unraveled the fate of Joan, Michelle, and Christy.

On the morning of June 1st, they embarked on their journey, departing Orlando and heading toward Tampa. However, upon their arrival in Tampa, they encountered difficulties finding their motel. Joe pulled over to the side of the road and retrieved a brochure with a map, attempting to orient herself. As she was engrossed in studying the map, a man approached their car.

The man, an unassuming figure in his

30s with blonde hair and a moustache, introduced himself and noticed their Ohio license plates. He offered his assistance, recognizing they were lost. Joe explained their predicament, and the man generously volunteered to provide directions to their motel. She handed him the brochure and a pen, and he jotted down the instructions for her. He also extended an invitation for them to join him on his boat that evening to watch the sunset, which they gladly accepted.

Before leaving, the man emphasized that his boat was blue and white. Joe took note of this, writing "blue with white" on the brochure as a reminder. Grateful for his help and excited about their boat trip, they continued following the man's directions to their motel. Arriving at approximately 12:30 p.m., they checked in. Their afternoon activities remain unclear, whether they spent time at the beach or a park, but they were spotted leaving the motel's restaurant at 7:30 p.m.

Later that evening, they returned to their room to prepare for the boat trip. They put on their bathing suits, shorts, and jackets. Michelle posed for a photo as she crouched down while getting ready, and they also took a snapshot of the view from their balcony, capturing the sunset over Tampa Bay.

Fully prepared, they proceeded to their car, with Joe driving them to the nearby public boat ramp. They spotted a blue and white boat, and the man was there, waving to them. Sometime between 8:30 and 9 p.m., they boarded the boat, ready for their adventure. However, the pleasantries quickly took a horrific turn.

The man, who had initially appeared friendly, turned violent. With little certainty about the exact sequence of events, it is evident that he assaulted all three women. Afterward, he bound their arms and ankles and placed duct tape over their mouths, leaving their eyes uncovered—forcing them to witness the unfolding nightmare.

The man retrieved three 30-pound cinder blocks from his boat and set them on the deck in front of the helpless women. With methodical precision, he attached ropes to the cinder blocks, forming nooses at the other ends. The horror escalated as he forced the women, one by one, to stand, secured the nooses around their necks, and attached the cinder blocks.

One by one, they were pushed overboard into the water, the cinder blocks pulling them down as they struggled. The remaining woman had to witness the harrowing demise of her loved ones, each struggling for life before sinking beneath the surface. After committing these heinous acts, the man calmly returned to the shore as if nothing had happened.

Then, on June 4th, three days after the tragic incident, the bloated bodies of the women surfaced due to decomposition. Despite the advanced state of decay, the autopsy revealed water in their lungs, confirming that they were alive when thrown into the water.

A few days later, when Joe's car and the notes inside it were discovered near the boat ramp, law enforcement started piecing together the puzzle. Speculation arose that Joe and her daughters had potentially boarded a boat before their disappearance. The grim realization dawned that these missing women were likely the same individuals whose unidentified bodies had been recovered in the bay a few days earlier.

As this connection was made, the police contacted Hal back in Ohio, requesting dental records to confirm the identities of his wife and daughters. Regrettably, the records confirmed his worst fears: his entire family was gone. The perpetrator responsible for this horrific tragedy was a man named Oba Chandler. A suspected serial killer, Chandler was known for boasting about his encounter with three women.

In 1994, Chandler was found guilty of murdering all three Rogers women. However, he never admitted guilt or exhibited any remorse. For nearly two decades, he languished on death row, devoid of any visitors, be it friends or family, as no one wanted to associate with him.

Finally, a little after 4 p.m. on November 17, 2011—approximately 22 years after Chandler's heinous act—he was led into the execution chamber at Florida State Prison. Secured to the gurney, a curtain was drawn aside to reveal him to the witnesses. Among them, Hal Rogers watched resolutely from the front row as the man who had shattered his life, Oba Chandler, faced the ultimate penalty of lethal injection.

"LEAP OF COURAGE: A TALE OF SACRIFICE AND SURVIVAL"

On August 1st, 2009, David Hartsock, a 44-year-old skydiving instructor, arrived at Skydive Houston's parking lot in Texas and proceeded inside. Shortly thereafter, like his fellow colleagues, Dave immersed himself in prepping for the day's activities before the facility opened for the expected weekend rush. Situated about 30 miles northwest of Houston in Waller, Skydive Houston's main facility nestled adjacent to a sprawling open airfield, resembling a vast green grass expanse. The facility consisted of multiple substantial structures, including a massive hangar that housed the Super Twin Otter airplanes, the aircraft used to transport skydivers for their jumps.

The offering of tandem jumping was a particular draw at Skydive Houston, especially appealing to first-time jumpers. Tandem jumping involved a skydiving student being securely fastened to the front of an instructor, enabling them to jump together from the plane. The instructor would guide the student throughout the jump, from maintaining stability in the air to deploying the parachute and landing safely. Dave had recently completed an intensive three-year training course to become a certified skydiving instructor, although even before this, he had already accumulated an impressive record of over 800 jumps due to his deep love for the sport.

Dave's connection with skydiving had reshaped his life, offering a sense of purpose he hadn't found elsewhere. Prior to his skydiving journey, he led an unremarkable life, residing in a modest suburban Houston home. He worked various blue-collar jobs, including stints as a cook in chain restaurants, managing a grocery store, and working at a soda bottling plant. Despite being divorced and childless, Dave maintained a close circle of friends who enjoyed pastimes like frequenting bars, bowling, and playing darts.

As Dave entered his forties, a growing sense of unfulfillment gnawed at him, prompting him to seek meaningful experiences. In 2004, after his divorce, a close friend invited him to skydive as a celebration for the friend's 40th birthday. Dave seized this opportunity to infuse his life with significance and agreed wholeheartedly. Following that initial jump, Dave found himself captivated. The exhilaration of plummeting through the sky at speeds exceeding a hundred miles per hour made all other concerns seem trivial. Skydiving introduced a sense of purity and elegance to his existence.

Dave's frequent visits to Skydive Houston over the years caught the attention of the manager. Recognizing Dave's dedication, the manager extended an offer for him to become a skydiving instructor. This transition marked a pivotal moment in Dave's life, as he left his position at the soda bottling plant to embark on a career that resonated deeply with his passion.

August 1st, 2009, fell on a Saturday, a day that typically saw Skydive Houston bustling with non-stop tandem jumps.

When Dave wasn't on the clock, managing solo jumps meant he could meticulously pack his own parachute, as he often did to ensure its proper configuration. Yet, during his work hours, especially during busy Saturdays, the constant back-and-forth of jumps didn't afford him the luxury of unpacking and repacking his chute each time. With continuous tandem jumps, Dave frequently resorted to using pre-packed parachutes available to instructors in their clubhouse.

As the day unfolded, Dave found himself ascending repeatedly with different students, executing jumps, deploying chutes, and touching down safely. As the clock neared four o'clock, Dave was getting ready to call it a day. His manager approached him with a request, "Could you manage one more tandem jump?" Despite the fatigue from the sweltering heat, despite the sweat streaming down, and despite already completing six jumps, Dave responded with his trademark simplicity, "No problem."

And so, his manager introduced Dave to a short, blonde woman named Shirley Dygert, who displayed visible signs of nervousness. Shirley's intention was to celebrate her 54th birthday by experiencing her first skydive. Alongside her were her husband, son, and three grandchildren, all eagerly waiting on the ground to watch her leap and commemorate the occasion. Furthermore, her other son, marking his 30th birthday, also planned to take to the skies.

Approaching Shirley, Dave flashed a reassuring smile and extended his hand, delivering a familiar line he often used with first-time jumpers. He quipped, "Don't worry, you'll be just fine. You'll be strapped to me, and I'm not about to let anything happen to myself." Shirley chuckled, her tension slightly easing. With a comforting pat on her shoulder, Dave walked over to the wall and retrieved one of the pre-packed parachutes. These specialized chutes contained two parachutes within the backpack: the main chute for regular deployment and the smaller reserve chute reserved for emergencies. The main chute is repacked after every jump, while the reserve chute remains packed due to its rarity of use. Certified technicians routinely test the reserve chutes, a practice standard across skydiving facilities, including Skydive Houston.

Equipped with the pre-packed parachute, Dave returned to Shirley, who was preparing in the staging area, outfitted in a flight suit resembling an adult onesie. Dave inspected and adjusted her suit before signaling to Shirley and her son to follow him. Exiting the staging area, the trio made their way to the airfield, where a Super Twin Otter airplane was idling. Other jumpers were already boarding the plane, eager for their own leaps. Joining the line, Dave, Shirley, and her son entered the plane, and within minutes, they were airborne. The aircraft ascended gradually to the jump altitude of 13,500 feet.

Seated in the airplane, Shirley occupied the bench seat directly in front of Dave, positioned at the back right of the compact aircraft. Sensing Shirley's nerves, Dave took the initiative to strike up a conversation, his inquiries delving into her background and occupation. In response, Shirley revealed that their lives were anchored in a rural Texas town, where she worked as a mail carrier, while her husband was employed in a mine. Their daily routines revolved around simplicity and a certain sense of monotony. As the conversation flowed, Shirley shared that the prospect of participating in skydiving was a departure from her norm. She disclosed that when her other son had voiced an interest in trying skydiving a year earlier, she had been resolutely opposed, deeming it far too dangerous. However, a shift in perspective had occurred recently within Shirley, as both she and her husband embraced a desire for more daring and adventurous experiences in their lives.

Around 20 minutes after take-off, all the tandem jumpers, including Shirley and Dave, were securely attached to their instructors. With Shirley harnessed to Dave, the plane reached the jump altitude of 13,500 feet. The side door of the plane was slid open, indicating that it was time to jump. Shirley's son was the first to jump, and Shirley shouted out to him from the back of the plane, "Have a good jump! I'll see you on the ground." As he and his instructor leaped out, they disappeared into the sky below.

Next in line was Shirley. Dave calmly instructed her to stand up, and they rose beside their bench. Before moving toward the exit, Dave, with a sense of muscle memory, ensured once again that he was securely fastened to Shirley. He tapped his rip cord behind him and checked his equipment, reassuring himself. Feeling prepared, he said to Shirley, "Okay, Shirley, let's go." Together, they made their way to the front of the plane, where the door was wide open. Positioned on the edge, Shirley's feet hung outside, gazing into the expansive sky. Amid the loud wind, Dave's voice was close to Shirley's ear, guiding her. He gently pulled Shirley's head back, directing her gaze upward to prevent her from looking down, which could induce panic in some individuals upon seeing the ground below. With Shirley's head now back, Dave calmly counted, "One, two, three." With grace, the two of them leapt out into the sky.

From the moment an individual jumps out of a plane at thirteen thousand five hundred feet, until the point of touching the ground, it takes perhaps two to three minutes, with about 30 seconds to a minute of actual free fall. However, those two to three minutes are so intense that they feel as though they stretch for 20 minutes. This was the aspect of skydiving that Dave cherished so deeply – the overwhelming presence and being truly in the moment. There's nothing else that can occupy your thoughts; it's just you hurtling through the sky towards the Earth. It's an incredible sensation. Dave had encountered several close calls in his life. A few years prior, he had been involved in a motorcycle accident where he was struck by a car, resulting in a fractured skull. Not long after that incident, he was in another accident that led to a fractured spine. Despite facing these challenges, Dave's singular thought was always, "I hope I can skydive again." Remarkably, he managed to make full recoveries and return to skydiving each time. Consequently, whenever he leaped out of a plane, an overwhelming sense of gratitude and fortune washed over him.

The plan for that evening's jump was for Dave to rotate them 360 degrees three separate times, allowing Shirley to get a comprehensive view down across Houston and all over Texas. When Dave noticed they were at five thousand feet, he used his wrist altimeter, which functions like a watch, to determine the altitude from the ground. At this point, Dave would pull the ripcord, deploying the main chute, and they would gradually descend to the ground. Initially, the jump proceeded as planned. After exiting the plane, they achieved a stable horizontal position with Shirley in front, her abdomen facing the ground, and Dave positioned directly behind her, controlling the skydive. After a brief moment, Dave slightly adjusted their orientation and began the rotation to provide Shirley with a panoramic view of the city. The breathtaking scene was complemented by the sensation of falling through the sky, which, despite reaching speeds exceeding 120 miles per hour due to terminal velocity, created an illusion of being gently lifted by the air.

As a first-time skydiver, Shirley absorbed the incredible experience with wonder, while even Dave, with his extensive skydiving history, found himself thoroughly enjoying the moment. However, Dave's primary focus was on his altimeter, as he needed to pull the parachute at 5000 feet. Carefully monitoring his altimeter, Dave finally spotted the altitude reading of 5000 feet. After quickly scanning his surroundings for other jumpers and confirming a clear path, he reached back and pulled the ripcord handle to deploy his main chute.

Typically, upon deploying the main parachute, there is a gradual unfurling process, avoiding a sudden jolt. However, in this instance, as soon as Dave pulled the ripcord handle, there was an abrupt yank on the parachute backpack, causing it to move away from him swiftly. Furthermore, a loud popping sound resonated from above.

Dave, relying on his extensive skydiving experience, promptly realized that something was wrong – and he was correct. The main parachute had indeed deployed from the backpack; however, it became entangled during its release, preventing it from inflating at all.

This unforeseen complication not only failed to decelerate their descent but also resulted in the entangled parachute acting as a sail, forcefully tilting Dave and Shirley to the side and initiating a perilous spiral known as a death spiral. This menacing rotation, characterized by an astonishing speed, typically leads to unconsciousness due to its intensity. Yet, Dave's seasoned expertise in skydiving allowed him to maintain composure, trying to guide his way out of the fatal spin by extending his limbs to establish a straight trajectory. Regrettably, his efforts proved futile; the spinning persisted with growing velocity.

Shirley, her consciousness nearly slipping away, cried out in bewilderment, seeking an explanation from Dave. Amid the chaotic whirl, Dave remembered possessing two knives that might offer a solution. With determination, he reached for the first knife. Regrettably, the tangled parachute lines obstructed his access to it, rendering it unattainable. The height was dwindling below 5,000 feet, then rapidly nearing 4,000, and on a direct course toward 3,000 feet. Amidst the relentless spin and mounting urgency, the first knife remained elusive.

The pair found themselves in dire straits: plummeting altitude, tangled parachute, and dwindling options. Remaining composed, Dave strained to grasp the second knife, situated within Shirley's reach. The furious spin thwarted his attempt to retrieve it, frustratingly just out of his grasp. The ground was rapidly approaching 2000 feet, so without alternative avenues, Dave initiated the deployment of the reserve parachute, acknowledging the impending clash with the tangled mess above them. The reserve chute engaged, inducing a gradual deceleration that initially infused hope into the desperate situation. The calamitous spin began to subside.

However, a nightmarish sequence of events ensued, confounding Dave's expectations. As the reserve parachute stabilized their descent, the main parachute caught a rush of heated air, inflating abruptly alongside the reserve. The resultant entanglement of two distinct parachutes caused a catastrophic aerodynamic configuration, resembling wings extending horizontally on either side. Tragically, this configuration, referred to as a down plane, functions as an accelerant, propelling jumpers uncontrollably toward the ground. Extricating oneself from a down plane is a daunting task due to the amplified inflation induced by the resulting velocity.

Aware of the grim situation, Dave recognized their perilous height—less than 2,000 feet. Instinctively, he exerted herculean effort to disentangle the parachutes from the down plane. Against tremendous odds, he succeeded, breaking free from the life-threatening spin. Unfortunately, both parachutes collapsed, and the ensuing consequence was a free fall from over

1,000 feet above the earth's surface, hurtling at speeds exceeding 100 miles per hour, helpless against the impending impact.

At this moment, Shirley is crying and screaming, not knowing what's happening. In contrast, Dave experiences an incredible sense of calm. Years ago, Dave had given up on the idea of ever having a family or children. He was a genuinely good person who would have been a great father, but it just wasn't in the cards for him. Instead, Dave had found solace in skydiving. Often, he would stay late at Skydive Houston, sitting around the campfire with other instructors and jumpers, sharing stories, having beers, and enjoying burgers. Sometimes, Dave would even spend the night at Skydive Houston, avoiding his empty three-bedroom house where all he wanted to do was skydive again. However, now, with the certainty of impending death, knowing it could happen any second, his thoughts were solely on Shirley.

Dave didn't care if he died. He felt that he had found his purpose, and if he were to die doing what he loved, so be it. However, the stakes were much higher for Shirley. Her family was watching her from the ground, and if he didn't act quickly, they would witness Shirley's tragic death. Dave couldn't bear the thought. He realized he had to do something to protect Shirley.

With only a few hundred feet left until impact, Dave yelled to Shirley, "Tuck your knees up!" Shirley immediately complied, bringing her knees up. Simultaneously, Dave pulled back with all his strength on the risers and toggles, attempting to switch positions with Shirley. With Shirley in front, her body would hit the ground first. Dave maneuvered them so that his back would hit the ground first. He was willing to sacrifice himself to save Shirley when impact came.

The reverberations of that impact echoed through the air. The impact resonated far beyond the immediate vicinity. People located a quarter mile away heard the deafening crash as their bodies hit the ground.

Upon impact, Shirley's entire family, who had been watching from the ground, witnessed the harrowing event. Their hearts raced as they saw the catastrophe unfold before their eyes. Shock and fear gripped them as they comprehended the severity of what had just happened. Without hesitation, everyone rushed over to the crash site, their concern and urgency propelling them forward.

The chaos of entangled bodies and wreckage met their eyes as they arrived. Staring at the scene in disbelief, their attention was immediately drawn to a remarkable sight – movement amidst the wreckage. It was Shirley, defying all odds by still being alive.

Paramedics arrived and proceeded to detach her from Dave's body. They swiftly transported her to the hospital, where she was found to have suffered serious injuries, including multiple broken vertebrae and significant internal damage. Although these injuries were severe, they weren't life-threatening. Shirley would ultimately survive.

Three days following her hospitalization, Shirley received devastating news. Dave, who had been brought to the hospital alongside Shirley, had also succumbed to his injuries and passed away. Dave's last-ditch maneuver had indeed worked; he managed to save Shirley's life, but it came at the cost of his own.

However, not long after Shirley and her family had been informed of Dave's death, another call reached them, this time to correct the earlier information. Dave was not dead; however, he was paralyzed from the neck down. A few weeks later, after Shirley was discharged from the hospital, she made her way to the Intensive Care Unit where Dave was receiving treatment. It was their first meeting since the accident. Dave was seated in a wheelchair, surrounded by tubes and wires. Upon seeing Shirley, he began to cry. As Shirley approached him, she gave him a hug and uttered the words, "I love you."

Today, Dave and Shirley maintain their friendship. Shirley has made a full recovery thanks to Dave's courageous action. Unfortunately, Dave remains paralyzed, possessing only limited sensation in his right arm. He currently resides in Texas with his mother, who provides full-time care for him.

"BENEATH THE SMILE: A TALE OF DECEIT, GRIEF, AND DEADLY SECRETS"

On the evening of March 3rd, 2022, at approximately 9 PM, Corey Richins, a 31-year-old woman, carefully settled her three young sons into their beds. With her children finally asleep, she descended the stairs of their opulent suburban Utah home to reach the kitchen. Once there, she called out for her husband, Eric, to join her. Corey had an exhilarating piece of news to share—news that had only come her way that day. Now that their children were peacefully asleep, she and her husband could revel in this revelation and enjoy a drink together.

A short while later, Eric entered the kitchen, and Corey greeted him with a warm smile. She handed him his drink, a subtle gesture marking the commencement of their private celebration. Without words, she conveyed her intent for them to adjourn to their bedroom upstairs. As they settled on their bed, Corey finally unveiled the grand news. Her modest real estate company had learned earlier that day that they were on the brink of finalizing a deal for an exquisite 20,000-square-foot mansion in Utah, with an asking price of two million dollars. Corey's shrewd calculations indicated that, after some strategic renovations, she could resell the property for three million dollars—an impressive one-million-dollar profit.

For years, Corey had invested relentless effort into her real estate venture, striving for a breakthrough. This development marked a pivotal milestone for her. However, their dwelling in a conservative corner of Utah implied certain societal expectations: Corey was supposed to play the role of a devoted homemaker, tending to their children and maintaining the household. Yet, Corey aspired to more than that. She harbored ambitions of a thriving professional career, one that could rival her husband's accomplishments.

Eric operated a lucrative masonry business, affording the family indulgent vacations and a lavish property in a cul-de-sac. Their children, aged five, seven, and nine, were no longer as dependent, as they had a nanny now. This change allowed Corey to finally chase her career dreams while still being present for her sons.

The couple, now seated on their bed, clinked their glasses together, savoring the moment and envisioning a future enriched by their newfound financial prospects. As they reviewed the details and imagined the enhanced lifestyle that awaited them, fatigue began to set in. Particularly for Eric, who had undergone an allergy shot earlier that day, leaving him weary and weak. Their energy waned, prompting them to decide to retire for the night.

After the routine of brushing their teeth and changing, Corey and Eric slipped beneath the covers and turned off the light. Their plans to embrace slumber were briefly interrupted by their seven-year-old son's cries from his bedroom. Slightly irritated, Corey stood, indicating she would address the issue. It was not uncommon for their son to have nightmares, and only her presence could comfort him.

Kissing Eric, Corey exited the room and proceeded down the hall to her son's bedroom. Once he was settled, she returned to her own room, nestling beside her husband. The calm of the night was disrupted a few hours later, around 3 AM, when Corey abruptly sat up in her son's bed. She momentarily grappled with confusion before realizing where she was. The house was enveloped in silence, yet Corey's unease grew. Her recollection of tending to her son brought her back to the present.

She checked her son to ensure he was asleep before returning to her own bed. However, a peculiar sensation gripped her as she settled beside Eric—his body felt alarmingly cold. Alarmed and unsettled, Corey roused him, hoping to decipher the cause of his chilling state. But Eric remained motionless, his weight heavy and unresponsive. Panic took hold as Corey repeatedly called his name, met with only chilling silence.

Leaping out of bed, Corey reached for her phone and dialed 911, frantic and in shock. As she described the situation to the dispatcher, the sound of approaching sirens provided a glimmer of relief. Paramedics rushed in, offering immediate assistance. Yet, as they assessed Eric, it was evident that his life had already slipped away.

The investigation into Eric's sudden demise commenced, baffling both Corey and authorities. An old painkiller pill bottle found near his bedside led to initial suspicions, but the label indicated it had long been empty. Corey recounted that Eric had recently received an allergy shot, hinting at a potential adverse reaction. Still, the notion that an allergy shot could result in his death seemed implausible.

While suicide was considered, Eric's character and circumstances didn't align with such a tragic outcome. A loving father, an active outdoorsman, and a devoted husband, he had a life full of joy, purpose, and professional success. The police launched a thorough inquiry, promising Corey answers, yet all she could think of were her three sons, peacefully unaware that their father was now gone forever.

In the ensuing weeks, as the family awaited autopsy results, Corey channeled her energy towards her three boys, who were profoundly impacted by the loss of their father. Eric had been an involved and hands-on parent, and the void he left was keenly felt in their lives. The youngest, a five-year-old, constantly inquired about his father's whereabouts and when they could see him again. The older two boys, who grasped the reality of their father's passing, posed poignant questions: Could Dad still see or hear them? Corey's heart ached in response, as she lacked the required answers.

Determined to aid her sons' grieving process, Corey sought out children's books that addressed grief, hoping these resources could provide solace. However, the books proved ineffective in assuaging their pain. Frustrated by this, Corey took a new approach a few weeks after Eric's passing, when the mystery surrounding his death still loomed. Gathering her sons, she began narrating an imaginative tale about their father, depicting him as an angel watching over them. Using crayons and paper, Corey sketched illustrations of their angelic father with wings and a halo, showing the boys down below, waving up at him. Through these stories, she conveyed that their dad was now their guardian angel, always listening, loving, and watching over them.

This narrative approach resonated deeply with the boys, forging a connection that helped them acknowledge their father's absence while preserving a meaningful bond. This storytelling became a nightly ritual, providing a much-needed avenue for processing grief.

As the days and weeks passed without answers or closure about Eric's death, Corey had an epiphany. The impact of these stories on her own children made her realize their potential to assist other families navigating loss. Inspired by this insight, she decided to transform these narratives and accompanying illustrations into a genuine children's grief book. Corey recognized the dearth of effective grief resources in the market and saw the potential to provide solace to countless families grappling with similar experiences.

On April 13th, six weeks following

Eric's passing and after the family had begun compiling their stories and illustrations into a kids' grief book, Corey was backing out of her driveway. At the other end of the cul-de-sac, she spotted a police car approaching—a familiar sight. It was Detective Woody, the lead investigator on Eric's case.

As the detective's car approached, Corey noticed his wave, signaling her to halt. She parked her car and quickly approached him. Detective Woody's serious expression was evident as he stepped out of his car and began to share the unsettling news he had for her. Recognizing the gravity of the situation, he conveyed that the autopsy results were in. Eric's cause of death wasn't natural—it was a fentanyl overdose. Fentanyl, a potent opioid frequently mixed with heroin, can be fatal even in minute quantities. Shocked and bewildered, Corey protested, asserting that Eric didn't use drugs other than the occasional marijuana gummy before bed. The detective was empathetic, understanding her disbelief but emphasizing that the results were conclusive.

Detective Woody informed Corey that

their next step would involve investigating any electronic communications Eric might have had regarding the fentanyl. Corey agreed to cooperate, consenting to the search of their devices. However, her memory triggered a crucial detail: Eric's business partner, Cody Wright, had taken Eric's laptop shortly after his passing. This raised suspicion in Corey's mind, as her interactions with Cody had revealed tensions between him and her late husband.

Corey divulged that Eric and Cody had been close friends who co-founded their masonry business years ago. However, their relationship soured after a hunting trip during which Cody reported Eric's illegal hunting activities to game wardens. Despite the strained partnership, they managed to continue their business endeavors, albeit with significant strain. Corey suggested that Cody might hold pertinent information and advised the detective to speak with him and retrieve Eric's laptop from him.

Detective Woody expressed gratitude for the information, promising to follow up with Cody and recover the laptop. With that, he thanked Corey and assured her they would stay in touch. Following this conversation, the investigation seemed to hit a roadblock. The dialogue with Cody didn't yield substantial leads, and new information about Eric's death or his connection to fentanyl remained elusive. The investigation appeared to stall, leaving the family waiting for answers.

Corey directed her energy towards her three boys, focusing on nurturing them through their grief. Collaborating on the children's grief book with them, she found a meaningful outlet amid the uncertainty surrounding Eric's demise.

On March 5th, 2023, nearly a year after Eric's passing and with no resolution in sight, the grief book was finally completed. Self-published on Amazon under the title "Are You with Me," the book resonated profoundly with parents seeking support for their grieving children. As rave reviews flooded in, local media took notice, leading to numerous interview requests for Corey. Although initially hesitant, Corey recognized the significance of sharing their journey and agreed to the interviews, propelled by the pride she felt for what she and her children had created. She was confident Eric would share in this sentiment.

Unbeknownst to Corey, the book's release triggered an unforeseen cascade of events. Ever since Eric's death in 2022, Utah police had meticulously scoured the electronic devices owned by both the Richins family and Eric's business partner, Cody. Their intent was to uncover any trace of communication between Eric and the individual responsible for his fatal fentanyl overdose. During this investigation, the police stumbled upon something unusual evidence that seemed linked to Eric's death. However, lacking concrete proof, they had no choice but to await further developments.

The increased media coverage surrounding Corey's grief book also highlighted the unresolved nature of Eric's demise. In response, several individuals who closely followed these news reports reached out to the police, asserting that Eric hadn't died from an accidental fentanyl overdose; he had been murdered. Some even claimed to know the identity of the alleged killer. Intriguingly, this suspect matched the person the Utah police had grown suspicious of due to the anomalies discovered during the electronic device searches.

On May 8th, 2023, fueled by these new leads, the Utah police felt they had amassed sufficient evidence to move forward. Armed with this newfound information, they embarked on a mission to apprehend the alleged killer, marking a critical turning point in the investigation.

While the full details of the case remain uncertain due to its ongoing status and the fact that the trial is yet to take place, according to prosecutors, the events leading to Eric Richards' death on March 3rd, 2022, are as follows:

On that fateful night, Eric was upstairs when he heard Corey's voice calling him from the kitchen. Intrigued, he descended the stairs to find his wife, Corey, with a radiant smile. She handed him a drink, revealing that she had exciting news to share and that they were going to celebrate. Afterward, the couple retreated to their bedroom, where Corey divulged the promising real estate deal that could earn their company a million-dollar profit. Raising their glasses in a toast, they took a sip from their Moscow Mule cocktails—a concoction of ginger beer, vodka, and lime.

However, unbeknownst to Eric, Corey had introduced a sinister ingredient into his drink: a fatal dose of fentanyl. Corey's motive behind this calculated act was rooted in a web of deceit. She had been embezzling funds from Eric's bank accounts, a fact that he had uncovered. Even more troubling, Eric had stumbled upon her taking out substantial loans under their family's name, causing him great distress. Determined to protect his assets from Corey's potential exploitation, Eric had decided to seek a divorce and had even begun consulting divorce lawyers. Faced with the looming threat of losing her source of wealth, Corey had coldly orchestrated a sinister plan, setting in motion a chain of events that would shatter their lives forever.

Sensing that her marriage was on the brink of collapse and her financial lifeline would be severed, Corey took out a two-million-dollar life insurance policy on Eric's life. With a chilling disregard for human life, she callously proceeded to end his life herself. Shortly thereafter, in a chilling twist,

Corey authored a grief book purportedly aimed at helping her sons cope with the loss of their father—a father she had taken from them.

Prosecutors allege that Corey had been plotting for weeks to determine the appropriate lethal dose of fentanyl. In a prior attempt on Valentine's Day, Corey had laced a sandwich with fentanyl and attached a note professing love. However, this attempt failed, resulting in Eric experiencing hives rather than succumbing to the poison. Undeterred, Corey intensified her efforts and eventually succeeded in administering a fatal dose of fentanyl through Eric's drink on March 3rd.

When First Responders arrived, Corey recounted a different story to them in hopes of deceiving them. She described how they had shared the celebratory drink, retired to bed, and how she had briefly left to tend to her son. Upon returning around 3 a.m., she found Eric cold to the touch, prompting her to call 9-1-1. In reality, after poisoning her husband, Corey's actions were far from her fabricated account.

She paced around the house for hours, conducting searches on Google for topics such as how to erase electronic evidence and luxury prisons for the wealthy in America. These suspicious searches were part of the electronic activity that raised law enforcement's suspicions during their initial investigation. However, while these raised red flags, they weren't sufficient evidence to immediately arrest Corey.

As time passed, Corey's grief book gained traction, and Eric's family, repulsed by the narrative and suspecting Corey's involvement in Eric's death, urged the police to take a closer look at her. The family's concern intensified as Corey seemed to profit from Eric's demise, fueling their belief that Corey was responsible for his death. Acting on these tips, alongside Corey's unusual search history on the night of Eric's death, the police were able to amass enough evidence to arrest her on May 8, 2023.

Despite her protestations of innocence, Corey faces a grave situation. Charged with aggravated murder, a conviction could lead to the possibility of the death penalty. She currently remains in custody, denied bail as she awaits her trial. In the wake of these developments, Corey's book, "Are You with Me," has been removed from sale on Amazon. As the legal proceedings unfold, the truth behind Eric's death and Corey's involvement will be scrutinized and decided in the courtroom.

"THE SILENT MENACE: UNRAVELLING THE MYSTERY OF GLORIA RAMIREZ"

In the year 1994, a 31-year-old mother found herself rushed into a California emergency room, her heart rate dangerously elevated and her blood pressure plummeting. Struggling to breathe, she became yet another challenging case for the seasoned doctors and nurses accustomed to such critical situations. Swiftly, the medical team sprang into action, diligently working to stabilize her condition.

Amid the focused chaos of the emergency room, one doctor's trained eye caught something peculiar about the patient. However, before this observation could be shared with the rest of the medical staff, a sudden, jarring thud echoed through the trauma room. Shockingly, it was followed by another thud, then another, creating an unsettling rhythm of disturbances within the room. Panic ensued as screams joined the chorus of sounds, and within minutes, the entire hospital was evacuated.

On the night of February 19, 1994, the clock ticked towards 8 PM, casting its shadow on a man's heart-wrenching 9-1-1 call in Southern California. The urgency in his voice wasn't surprising to anyone familiar with Gloria Ramirez's plight. Gloria, his girlfriend, had recently been diagnosed with terminal cervical cancer, shattering their world just six weeks prior. Armed with this grim prognosis, she was prepared for her health to deteriorate rapidly, but nothing could prepare them for the events that unfolded that night.

As the 9-1-1 dispatcher picked up the

call, the man's voice trembled as he pleaded for an ambulance to be dispatched immediately. He knew the stakes were high; Gloria's life hung by a fragile thread. Despite the urgency, his demeanor wasn't one of surprise. After all, Gloria's battle with cancer had been a fierce one. Her journey had been marked by strength, resilience, and the determination to live life fully for her two children – a 9-year-old boy and a 12-year-old girl.

Gloria's love for her children was the driving force behind her will to survive. She cherished every moment spent with them, a beacon of joy in their lives. Whether it was laughter, homework assistance, or bonding through religious hymns, Gloria infused positivity into their days. This profound connection defined her, even extending beyond motherhood. Her cheerful demeanor was infectious, her presence uplifting, and her smile, a symbol of hope.

The diagnosis of terminal cancer hadn't deterred Gloria's spirit. Instead, it ignited a fierce determination to explore every avenue that could potentially alleviate her condition. With radiation treatment scheduled at the end of February, Gloria had a few weeks to explore options and hold onto her unwavering hope. However, on that pivotal February 19th evening, Gloria's breathing struggles triggered the call to 9-1-1. Her boyfriend, well-acquainted with Gloria's relentless willpower, knew that time was of the essence.

The ambulance arrived promptly at Gloria's home, rushing her to Riverside Hospital. In the ER, Dr Julie Gorchynski, a seasoned physician, took charge of Gloria's case. The urgency of the situation was familiar to Julie, who thrived in the fast-paced environment of the ER. The flurry of medical activity that followed aimed to stabilize Gloria's fluctuating heart rate and alarming blood pressure.

In the midst of treating Gloria, the medical team observed curious anomalies – a faint garlicky odor on Gloria's breath and an unusual greasiness on her skin. These details didn't escape their notice, although they were attributed to the urgency of the situation. The focus remained on stabilizing Gloria's condition as her heart rhythm fluctuated. Electric shocks were administered to her chest, a standard procedure to restore normal heartbeats.

During these efforts, a strange chemical smell pervaded the trauma room. Julie, fully engrossed in Gloria's case, immediately noticed the unusual odor and instinctively discussed it with her fellow colleagues. An eerie moment followed, creating a chilling ripple of unease throughout the medical team. Two nurses, standing in the room, suddenly collapsed, their health compromised by an invisible and potent menace.

As panic swiftly overtook the medical team, they watched in shock and disbelief as their colleagues succumbed to the mysterious threat, their bodies rendered incapacitated in a matter of moments. Amidst the chaos and confusion, Julie's awareness heightened. She discerned a strange and unsettling sight – crystalline formations within a vial containing Gloria's blood. Desperate to communicate her observation to her fellow colleagues, she fought against a mounting dizziness and nausea that threatened to overwhelm her.

Julie's strength wavered, and the room spun around her. Her vision blurred, and her body grew weak. Eventually, the overpowering sensations became too much, and Julie too collapsed.

As the situation spiraled out of control, hospital-wide evacuation was initiated, with only a skeletal medical crew remaining. Outside, the scene was chaotic, with ambulances, frantic patients, and medical personnel filling the parking lot. Gloria's condition, however, prevented her from being moved and required concentrated medical attention.

Inside the hospital, the trauma room saw a tragic culmination as Gloria's heart rate and blood pressure plummeted. Despite the team's best efforts, she passed away at approximately 8:50 PM, leaving a wake of medical staff who had also fallen ill. The incident prompted a hazardous materials response, as a mysterious chemical presence was suspected.

In the aftermath of that tumultuous night, a cloud of uncertainty loomed over the medical staff and patients of Riverside Hospital. The untimely passing of Gloria Ramirez had left not only questions but also a trail of unexplained symptoms and medical mysteries.

Amid the shroud of uncertainty, a prevailing theory emerged—an elusive leak within the hospital, stealthily infiltrating trauma room one, sowing the seeds of collapse and illness. Yet, despite an exhaustive search by the HazMat team, no evidence of this elusive toxin-laden breach surfaced. Authorities, perplexed but cautious, urged vigilance around the hospital and Gloria's body, lest some hidden venom lay dormant, a ticking time bomb.

Six days post the tragic incident, a hermetic chamber hosted an autopsy, where doctors, cloaked in protective suits, delved into the mysteries within Gloria. Astonishingly, the autopsy unveiled an unexpected truth—Gloria's demise had no sinister origins. Instead, her terminal cancer had orchestrated her heart and kidney failure, claiming her life with a somber, yet natural, finality.

The aftermath, far from neat, left Julie grappling with persistent health challenges. From breathlessness to the agony of pancreatitis, and bones gnawed away by an unrelenting decay, Julie's suffering became a testament to the inexplicable events of that night. While others began their journey to recovery, she was confined to a wheelchair, her body a canvas of torment.

As the dust settled, blame cast a dark shadow. Gloria's family harbored suspicions, pointing accusing fingers at Riverside Hospital. They contended that toxic fumes, lurking in trauma room one, were the malevolent puppeteers behind the staff's afflictions and Gloria's demise. An unsettling history of hazardous materials breaches within the hospital's walls lent credence to their assertions.

However, Riverside Hospital vehemently rejected culpability, asserting that no leaks or toxins were discovered within their premises. The complex narrative grew murkier, with extensive investigations yielding no toxic culprits. Amidst the courtroom battles and hospital accusations, the California Department of Human and Health Services offered an explanation that left many unsatisfied—mass sociogenic illness.

In this narrative, fear and anxiety wielded power, planting an illusion of sickness in the minds of both staff and patient. Julie and her fellow 22 stricken coworkers, it was suggested, had fallen victim to their collective imagination. As for Gloria, the department contended that her cancer was the sole agent of her demise.

Dissatisfaction resonated deeply within Gloria's grieving family and Julie. The theory of mass sociogenic illness clashed against Julie's well-documented medical struggles, rendering her unable to walk due to her deteriorating bones. Rejecting the notion of collective delusion, they resolved to seek justice through legal avenues, convinced that the hospital was concealing a more ominous truth.

In the middle of the legal battles and growing skepticism, an obscure lab on the outskirts of San Francisco, known as the Forensic Science Centre, stepped onto the stage. Their mission: to unravel the mystery that had eluded everyone's grasp. The pursuit of answers was far from over, and what these scientists would uncover would shatter preconceived notions and finally put the case to rest.

Following Gloria's cancer diagnosis,

she embarked on a relentless journey of research, delving not only into her own illness but also exploring alternative treatments she could administer independently. This tireless endeavor persisted until her scheduled radiation treatment, set to commence at the close of February. The scientists at the Forensic Science Centre would later unveil a critical element of this puzzle.

As per the revelations by the Forensic Science Centre, it appeared that Gloria had turned to a well-known yet controversial home remedy to alleviate her pain. The remedy in question was dimethyl sulfoxide, abbreviated as DMSO, which gained notoriety in the 1960s for its applications in treating pain and anxiety. Alas, as its popularity soared, its potential to induce eye damage emerged, leading to its prohibition by governmental authorities.

Even though DMSO was relegated from the realm of medical treatment, it continued to be available in gel form, found in hardware stores and marketed as a heavy-duty degreaser. In a twist of fate, Gloria had taken to applying this gel based DMSO generously across her skin, enveloping herself from head to toe. Thus, upon her arrival at the emergency room, her skin bore the telltale signs of greasiness, with an equally distinct garlic-like aroma emanating from her breath—an outcome of DMSO's peculiar interaction within the body.

Yet, the startling revelation of Gloria's use of DMSO failed to completely explain the cascade of collapses and illnesses that befell the hospital staff in her proximity. A deeper layer of intricacy emerged as it was discovered that on that pivotal night, Gloria harbored another medical condition, seemingly insignificant, yet harboring profound implications. Amidst her struggles with breathing, Gloria was also grappling with a urinary tract infection, a detail overlooked both by her boyfriend during the 9-1-1 call and by the attending paramedics.

While Gloria had the urinary tract infection, her body was unable to flush out the DMSO chemicals that had seeped into her system from the gel applied to her skin. It's worth noting that even when there are significant amounts of DMSO chemicals in the body or on the skin, they typically do not pose a danger to the person or those around them.

However, the danger came into play when the attending EMTs placed an oxygen mask on Gloria's face inside the ambulance. This seemingly routine action unintentionally set off a chain reaction. During Gloria's ambulance transport to the hospital, an unforeseen chemical reaction was set in motion. The experts at the Forensic Science Centre explained that the oxygen introduced into Gloria's system began to interact with the DMSO chemicals that were already present within her body due to the gel application.

For this catastrophic chain of events to unravel within the hospital, the precise occurrence of two specific events was imperative. The first pivotal event was the electric shocks administered during Gloria's resuscitation. In the analysis of experts, these electric charges assumed a role as a catalyst, sparking a transformative process within the chemical composition already present within Gloria's body. The outcome of this process was the conversion of the chemical into an unstable and hazardous form, thereby laying the foundation for the subsequent tragedy.

Secondly, an apparently routine procedure in any medical setting – the extraction of Gloria's blood by a nurse – held a hidden, devastating potential. Unbeknownst to the hospital staff, this seemingly innocuous action would prove to be the final catalyst for a near deadly outcome. As the unstable chemical was drawn out of Gloria's body and introduced into the cold environment of the hospital, a process of stabilization commenced. The chemical underwent a metamorphosis, evolving into crystalline formations, Eventually, this transformation led to the chemical assuming a gaseous state, diffusing into the surrounding air.

Despite the grim revelations, the catastrophic event did not factor into Gloria's ultimate demise, as she succumbed to her cancer. Yet, her family persisted in denying Gloria's use of DMSO, asserting that Riverside Hospital bore responsibility for her untimely passing. A substantial settlement was reached, albeit without the hospital admitting guilt. Julie's legal endeavors against the hospital were met with dismissal; however, her courage and resilience enabled her to rejoin the medical profession, her steadfast dedication fortified by the harrowing ordeal.

"DESCENT INTO TURBULENCE: THE ORDEAL OF FLIGHT 14"

On April 17, 2018, Holly Mackey, a 42-year-old woman, took her seat in aisle 14c aboard a Southwest Airlines plane. The aircraft was bound from New York City to Dallas, Texas, carrying a total of 143 passengers, along with five crew members. Holly's journey wasn't over at Dallas; she was set to continue to Oklahoma City, her home. She settled into her aisle seat, placed her carry-on under the seat in front of her, and patiently waited to see who her fellow seatmates would be.

Soon, a 43-year-old bank executive and

mother of two, Jennifer Reardon, approached Holly's row. With a cheerful smile, Jennifer inquired if the seats beside Holly were available, to which Holly confirmed. Open seating was the norm for Southwest Airlines, and Jennifer secured the window seat (14a) beside Holly. Both passengers fastened their seatbelts and stowed their carry-on bags.

As the flight continued boarding, middle seats remained unoccupied as passengers typically preferred window or aisle seats. Eventually, a pre-teen girl asked Holly if she could take the middle seat (14b) between her and Jennifer. Holly agreed, and the girl settled in, occupied with her phone.

With all the passengers in their seats, the flight attendants began the pre-flight safety procedures. Holly was among the few genuinely paying attention, sensing an unusual foreboding about the flight. She followed along closely, her intuition guiding her attention to the details. After the safety briefing, the flight attendant advised passengers to relax and enjoy the flight.

Despite the general lack of concern

from other passengers, Holly couldn't shake her unease. A combination of this unsettling feeling and the urge from a large cup of iced coffee pushed her attention towards the airplane's restroom. However, the plane had started its taxi to the runway, and she was told to remain seated until the aircraft reached cruising altitude.

As the plane accelerated on the runway, the powerful engines pushed Holly, Jennifer, and the girl back into their seats. They gazed out the window as the airport dwindled in the distance, and the plane ascended into the sky. Holly, feeling both mentally and physically uncomfortable, turned her attention inward, anticipating the moment when they would level off and the cabin would resound with that familiar chime, signaling it was safe to move about.

As the plane seemed to level out, indicating they might have reached cruising altitude soon, Holly pre-emptively unbuckled her seatbelt and turned toward the aisle, anticipating the chime that would signal the freedom to use the bathroom. But unexpectedly, no such chime sounded.

Instead, the captain's voice echoed through the intercom, informing everyone of reaching cruising altitude while cautioning them to remain in their seats due to anticipated turbulence ahead.

Feeling a mix of frustration and disappointment, Holly let out an audible grunt. Jennifer, who had been engrossed in her book, looked up in concern at Holly's reaction. As their eyes met, Holly explained her urgent need for the restroom, leading to a shared laugh between the two women over the ironic situation. With Jennifer's reassurance that she would likely be able to use the bathroom soon, Holly returned to her anxious wait, the girl seated between them still absorbed in her phone.

After some time, Holly began to worry that turbulence could potentially keep her confined to her seat. Watching the flight attendants securely fasten themselves in response to the turbulence and sensing her own growing unease, she opted to shift her focus to work. At 11:04 AM Eastern, she retrieved her laptop, feeling an increasing need to divert her attention from the mounting discomfort and unease.

However, just as she began to reach for her laptop, two deafening and rapid sounds shattered the cabin's calm. A loud popping noise emanated from outside the plane, near the left wing—right by their window. This was followed by a whooshing sound that filled the entire cabin, accompanied by an abrupt drop in temperature. The plane suddenly banked hard to the left.

In the chaotic aftermath, Holly snapped out of her shock. The cabin was filled with the hissing of deployed oxygen masks, screams of passengers, and the hurried footsteps of attendants. The plane's sharp banking to the left was causing mayhem among the passengers. Holly reached out, attempting to don the oxygen mask in front of her, but her trembling hands struggled to fit the band over her head. She felt a sense of helplessness and disbelief—this couldn't be how it would end.

Yet, as the panic surged, she regained her focus. Her initial struggle with the mask faded as she turned her attention toward her fellow passengers. In the midst of this turmoil, she saw something that chilled her to her core.

The disturbing popping noise Holly had heard had originated from the exploding engine beneath the plane's left wing. The violent explosion had shattered the cowling, sending a piece of debris crashing into the aircraft's side. This piece struck the window of row 14, the very window adjacent to Holly's seat. The impact resulted in the window fracturing completely, triggering a rapid and explosive decompression of the cabin. In an instant, hurricane-like forces surged through the plane, and the unsecured objects, including people, faced the ominous pull of the void beyond.

The immediate aftermath was a horrifying scene. The woman closest to the broken window, Jennifer, was violently pulled partway through it. Her upper body jutted out of the aircraft, held back only by her seatbelt. Meanwhile, the girl seated between Holly and Jennifer felt herself being dragged toward the window due to the powerful suction created by the breach.

Reacting on instinct, Holly reached out and clutched the girl, holding her tightly against her chest. With her other arm, she attempted to grasp Jennifer's seatbelt, attempting to pull her back into the cabin. Yet, the relentless forces were overpowering—Jennifer's body was firmly entrenched outside the plane. The surreal situation was beyond comprehension; the unthinkable was unfolding right before her eyes.

Struggling against the roaring noise and the sheer physical struggle, Holly screamed desperately, hoping for someone to notice their plight. The cabin was enveloped in pandemonium, with the noise drowning out individual cries for help. The plane's sharp bank to the left only intensified the chaos, with passengers consumed by fear and panic.

For agonizing moments, Holly clung to Jennifer and the girl, shouting for assistance that couldn't break through the cacophony. No matter how she waved or screamed, her efforts seemed futile. The urgency of their situation, coupled with the disorienting circumstances, hindered anyone's ability to help. As the minutes ticked by, Holly's desperation grew, but rescue remained elusive.

Eventually, the plane began to regain stability as the pilot fought to regain control. The turbulence eased slightly, and passengers cautiously opened their window shades, assessing their surroundings. A few noticed the dire situation in row 14 and raised the alarm. They shouted and gestured for the attention of the flight attendants, but the overpowering noise from the damaged window made their efforts futile.

The attendants were themselves preoccupied with the immediate concerns of managing the frightened passengers and coordinating with the pilot to address the crisis. Amidst the confusion and the din, the plight of Jennifer, Holly, and the girl went unnoticed. It was a surreal and disheartening realization—the desperation for help contrasted starkly with the overwhelming circumstances.

As the plane gradually regained a semblance of stability, the ordeal showed no signs of abating. Holly, still holding Jennifer and the girl, clung to them for dear life. Despite the futility of their situation, a sense of solidarity emerged among the passengers in the nearby rows. A woman in row 15 extended her hand in a gesture of empathy, gently touching Holly's back, wordlessly acknowledging the gravity of the situation.

In those heart-wrenching moments, the plane soared through the sky, its passengers facing a perilous combination of physical forces and emotional turmoil. The unfolding tragedy left Holly grappling with the realization that, despite their best efforts, Jennifer was likely already dead.

Captain Tammy Joe Schultz, a seasoned veteran of the airline, exhibited remarkable skill and composure. Despite the damaged left engine resulting from its explosion, she countered the sudden and severe bank to the left, eventually regaining control of the plane. Through the intercom system, her authoritative commands reached the flight attendants, enabling them to initiate assistance for the passengers.

Reacting swiftly, they promptly reseated Holly and the young girl to a more secure row. Displaying truly inspiring courage, two passengers, Andrew and Tim, fearlessly volunteered to make their way to row

14. Understanding the urgency of the situation, they faced the distressing circumstances with unwavering determination. Despite the imminent danger of being pulled out themselves, they orchestrated their efforts with synchronized strength to successfully bring Jennifer back into the cabin. They carefully positioned her in the aisle before calmly exiting the row without any harm.

With Jennifer now lying in the aisle, a nurse named Peggy, among the passengers, sprang into action. Peggy promptly began administering CPR, valiantly attempting to resuscitate Jennifer. As Holly glanced around the cabin, a sense of eerie calm had filled the plane. Despite the deafening noise emanating from the damaged window, an unsettling tranquility pervaded. Passengers remained seated; their attention fixed on the life-saving efforts taking place in the aisle.

At 11:21 AM, seventeen minutes after the initial engine explosion, the captain executed a skillful emergency landing at an airport in Philadelphia. Upon touchdown, a waiting medical team swiftly retrieved Jennifer from the plane, transporting her to a hospital.

Tragically, despite their valiant efforts, Jennifer succumbed to the severe injuries sustained during her ordeal. The fractured window and the violent expulsion from the plane had proven insurmountable.

The seemingly mundane events leading up to the crisis underscored the unpredictability of fate. Had circumstances aligned differently, Holly's journey might have taken a vastly divergent course. Instead, her altered seat choice placed her in proximity to Jennifer and subjected her to a life-altering ordeal. As the harrowing minutes passed, the unfathomable struggle for survival unfolded within the confines of row 14.

On the morning Holly boarded the plane, there's a detail that adds an even more traumatic layer to her experience. She had arrived at the airport quite early, with a large coffee in hand. While in line for security, she was sipping on her coffee. As she approached the security scanners, she finished the coffee and disposed of the cup. However, this took more time than expected, causing her to be late. Consequently, she rushed to her gate only to find her boarding group had already begun boarding. Her preferred seats towards the front were taken, and she settled for the first available row.

She walked down the aisle, searching for a vacant spot and finally arrived at row 14. On her left were three open seats, and in line with her routine on longer flights, she chose the window seat, 14a, as it allowed her to lean her head against the plane's side for better sleep. After fastening her seatbelt and placing her bag under the seat in front of her, she recalled the large coffee she had consumed during security. Although she didn't need to use the bathroom right then, she anticipated needing to go a couple of times after take-off.

Thinking ahead and not wanting to disturb her potential seatmates by repeatedly climbing over them to reach the restroom, Holly made a decision. She realized that although the window seat provided better sleep, the aisle seat would offer the convenience of easy restroom access without causing disruption. She unbuckled her seatbelt, retrieved her bag from under the seat, and moved two seats over to the aisle seat in row 14. Little did she know, this seemingly innocuous decision would unintentionally intertwine her destiny with Jennifer's.

"DARK WATERS: THE TRAGIC DISAPPEARANCE OF TOM AND JACKIE HAWKS"

In 1986, Tom Hawks found himself at a chili cook-off in Newport Beach, California, a 39-year-old father raising two teenage boys. Having been divorced from his sons' mother, Tom's life took an unexpected turn when he laid eyes on a captivating woman amidst the crowd. This woman, Jackie, 29 years old and radiantly beautiful, had him captivated from the start. Overcoming his initial embarrassment from getting caught in his gaze, Tom introduced himself and kindled a connection that rapidly evolved into deep affection. They fell head over heels in love, sharing stories, laughter, and dreams under the warm California sun. Eventually, this blossoming romance led to marriage in 1989, a union celebrated with joy by 150 of their closest friends and family members.

As an unfortunate motorcycle accident had left Jackie unable to bear children, the couple's joy was boundless when their sons found partners and one of them announced the impending arrival of a grandchild. Tom and Jackie reveled in the idea of embracing parenthood again, eager to extend their warmth and care to their upcoming grandbaby. Thus, they decided to sell their cherished yacht, the "Well-Deserved," The yacht had become a symbol of their adventures together, a vessel that had carried them along the mesmerizing coastline, where they watched sunsets melt into the ocean's horizon and created many memories over the years.

After selling the yacht to a young couple named Jennifer and her husband, Tom and Jackie intended to purchase a home closer to their family. It was a decision that marked a new chapter in their lives, embracing the role of grandparents and savoring the prospect of creating a nurturing environment for their grandchild.

However, shortly after sealing the yacht's sale, communication with Tom and Jackie ceased, raising concerns among their family and friends. Tom's brother, Jim, a retired police chief with a protective nature, embarked on a quest to uncover the truth.

Visiting the yacht, Jim encountered puzzling signs – loose lines, tarps askew, and abandoned belongings – that indicated Tom and Jackie's uncharacteristic departure. The once-vibrant vessel now stood as a silent witness to their absence, leaving behind an air of mystery.

Jim's inquiries revealed that Jennifer, the yacht's buyer, also struggled to reach the Hawks after encountering technical queries and finding personal items left behind. The yacht, which had been a cherished haven for Tom and Jackie, now held echoes of their sudden vanishing. Jennifer's experience added another layer to the puzzle, showcasing the abruptness of their departure and the challenges they faced in the aftermath of the sale.

Speaking with Jennifer, Jim learned that Tom and Jackie left promptly after completing the sale. The Hawks had spoken about plans to purchase a house near their son in Arizona, where a grandchild was on the way. As Jim delved further into their situation, he found no record of their recent activities or significant transactions. He enlisted Patricia, the couple's financial manager, to probe their accounts for large deposits, hoping to find a thread that would shed light on their whereabouts.

The unsettling realization that the couple had not deposited the substantial sale amount deepened concerns. Unable to pinpoint a reasonable explanation, Jim contacted the Newport Beach police to report Tom and Jackie as missing, setting off a chain of events to unravel the puzzle that surrounded their sudden disappearance.

Upon receiving the distressing news of Tom and Jackie Hawks' disappearance, the Newport Beach Police Department immediately swung into action. They recognized the urgency of the situation and understood that every moment counted in finding the missing couple.

The police's first step was to delve into the background of the new owners of the yacht, the Deleon's. Their investigation uncovered an unsettling fact about Skyler Deleon – a 25-year-old with a history of felony convictions, including armed robbery. This discovery added a layer of suspicion to the Deleon's' involvement in the Hawks' disappearance, making them prime subjects for further scrutiny.

A detective was dispatched to the dock where the yacht had been moored. The intention was to gather insights from the scene and hopefully stumble upon any clues that might shed light on the Hawks' whereabouts. As the detective approached the yacht, a peculiar mark caught their eye – what seemed to be a bloody handprint on one of the windows. This discovery sparked an urgency to secure a search warrant and thoroughly investigate the yacht for any potential evidence.

The subsequent search of the yacht was a meticulous process, with law enforcement officers combing through every nook and cranny in the hopes of discovering any clue that might offer a glimpse into the Hawks' final moments on the vessel. However, the search yielded no significant evidence or breakthroughs. This outcome left investigators frustrated and eager for more leads that might help unravel the mystery.

The authorities reached out to Skyler De Leon, urging him to come to the police station and provide a detailed account of his final interaction with the Hawks. Cooperatively, Skyler arrived at the police station and explained to the detectives how he had encountered an ad for a yacht in a fishing magazine. He had contacted Tom Hawk, expressing his interest. Subsequently, the two met up for a sea trial, akin to a test drive but for a boat. During the sea trial, Skyler conveyed his interest in purchasing the boat to Tom. On November 15th, Skyler, accompanied by his pregnant wife, young daughter, a notary, and a friend who acted as a witness, assembled in the parking lot near the yacht's dock. At this rendezvous point, the Hawks—Tom and Jackie—arrived.

In this meeting, Skyler and his group handed a suitcase filled with cash to Tom. The Hawks, accompanied by a notary, signed the necessary sale documents, officially transferring ownership of the yacht to the De

Leons. With the transaction complete, the Hawks received their suitcase of cash, boarded their SUV, and departed—likely headed to Mexico.

In response to the detectives' inquiry about how he could afford such an expensive vessel, Skyler initially provided a tale of having earned money as a child star during the 1990s. He claimed to have been an extra on the popular TV show "Power Rangers," accumulating enough funds to purchase the yacht. However, he abruptly corrected himself, admitting that this was not the truth. The reality, he confessed, was that the money used for the yacht purchase was obtained through theft.

He had been involved in stealing money from a drug kingpin before being arrested and sent to jail. During his time in jail, he had hidden the stolen money, only to retrieve it after his release. However, since the money was obtained through illegal means, it was considered "hot" and needed to be laundered. This led him to the decision of purchasing the yacht as a means to transform the illicit money into a legitimate asset. By buying the yacht with the bulk of cash, he aimed to convert the tainted money into a valuable possession, which he could then sell to acquire clean money.

Skyler's confession left the police astounded, as he had essentially confessed to participating in a money laundering scheme. Despite the gravity of his admission, the police decided not to charge him with money laundering due to his cooperative and forthcoming attitude during the investigation. Consequently, they released Skyler.

Continuing their investigation, the police interviewed Skyler's wife, Jennifer, the notary, and the friend who had witnessed the final boat sale. All three of them provided consistent descriptions of the event, recounting how they saw Tom and Jackie take the suitcase filled with cash, sign the paperwork, and then leave in their car. The only discrepancy lay in their observations of Tom and Jackie's behavior. While Skyler indicated that Tom seemed anxious and paranoid about the money, the notary mentioned that Tom and Jackie appeared completely normal to them.

After conducting interviews with those who had last seen Tom and Jackie, the police found themselves at an impasse, unsure of their next steps. Feeling stuck, they turned to the media, releasing a bulletin featuring images of Tom, Jackie, and their vehicle. The bulletin implored anyone with information to come forward. Within just a few days of the bulletin's broadcast, an older couple in Mexico contacted the authorities to report that the Hawks' SUV was parked across the street from their residence.

Both Mexican and American authorities swiftly responded, rushing to the location indicated by the couple. With a sense of anticipation, they approached the house where the SUV was parked, fully expecting to find either Tom and Jackie or someone familiar with them. However, their expectations were turned upside down when a man, completely unfamiliar to them, answered the door. The officers questioned him about the ownership of the parked SUV. In a state of confusion, the man replied that the vehicle belonged to his friend, Skyler De Leon.

This revelation was a pivotal moment. It exposed Skyler's deception to the authorities. Skyler had previously told the police that the last time he had seen Tom and Jackie, they had driven away in their SUV. However, this new information shattered that claim. It was evident that he had acquired their vehicle afterward and then handed it over to an unfamiliar person in Mexico. This discovery pointed towards a web of lies and complexities that further deepened the mystery surrounding the Hawks' disappearance.

Arrested for money laundering, Skyler was apprehended and questioned. A search of his residence uncovered items belonging to the Hawks, adding weight to the growing pile of evidence against him. Throughout the process, Skyler maintained his innocence, echoing his wife Jennifer's claims that their connection to the disappearance was purely coincidental. Despite their staunch denial, the police remained resolute in their conviction that Skyler was withholding key information.

The Newport Beach police leveraged Skyler's on-camera money laundering confession to apprehend him. He was arrested on charges of money laundering. With Skyler in custody, law enforcement obtained a search warrant for his and Jennifer's residence. The search yielded a significant discovery - various items that belonged to the Hawks, such as laptops and video cameras. These were belongings that Tom and Jackie would not have likely left behind on the yacht. Despite this compelling evidence linking Skyler to the Hawks' disappearance, he continued to assert his innocence, claiming it was all a misunderstanding.

While Skyler was being questioned by the police, his wife Jennifer echoed his stance, even appearing on talk shows to declare their innocence. She maintained that Skyler had no involvement in the Hawks' disappearance and that they were just as concerned about Tom and Jackie as everyone else. However, the police remained skeptical. They were convinced that Skyler was withholding crucial information.

In their pursuit of answers, the police decided to re-interview the notary and the friend who had acted as a witness during the final sale of the boat. The notary, Kathleen Harris, was brought back to the police department. Despite her previously unblemished record, Kathleen eventually cracked under intense questioning. She admitted that she had never met Tom and Jackie in her life. Instead, she confessed that Skyler had paid her a substantial sum of money upfront in cash to retroactively date the sale documents that had already been signed.

Similar rigorous interrogation was directed at Alonso Mation, the friend who had witnessed the sale. Initially adhering to Skyler's version of events, Alonso crumbled under scrutiny. Confronted with irrefutable evidence of Kathleen's admission, Alonso opted to cooperate in exchange for a reduced sentence. This agreement marked a pivotal moment in the investigation, finally poised to uncover the elusive truth behind the Hawks' disappearance.

Alonso was a young man, easily influenced and in his early to mid-20s. He had crossed paths with Skyler while the latter was incarcerated for his armed robbery conviction. Despite the unlikely circumstances of their meeting, Skyler and Alonso struck up an unexpected friendship. Their bond grew, leading to countless hours spent together. It was during November of 2004 when Skyler revealed his darkest secret to Alonso. He confessed that he was an international assassin, claiming to target only those who deserved it. Skyler disclosed to Alonso that he had a current contract to eliminate two individuals – Tom and Jackie Hawks. However, Skyler didn't intend to carry out this task alone; he offered Alonso the opportunity to be part of the operation, promising him a staggering reward of 1 million U.S. dollars.

Seeing the potential for unimaginable wealth, Alonso agreed to participate. On November 15th, the plan was set into motion. Skyler, Alonso, and another recruited accomplice named John Kennedy gathered at the dock's parking lot. Contrary to the assumption that the meeting was for finalizing the yacht's sale, they were actually there to perform a sea trial, a test voyage to evaluate the yacht's performance. A sea trial would allow Skyler's plan to unfold without drawing undue attention.

However, upon encountering Tom and Jackie Hawks, the situation quickly escalated. Tom, a seasoned probation officer, immediately sensed danger emanating from the trio. The atmosphere was tense, and Tom even suggested postponing the trial due to his unease. At this juncture, Skyler made a strategic move – he pretended to receive a phone call, allowing Jennifer (his wife) to arrive with their one-year-old daughter. Jennifer's presence transformed the mood entirely. Jackie, captivated by the child, was at ease, and Tom's reservations began to waver. He agreed to proceed with the sea trial, convinced that they were among friendly individuals.

As the group made their way onto the "Well Deserved" for the sea trial, a sudden turn of events unfolded. Just before embarking, Jennifer expressed her inability to join due to her baby being upset. She opted to go home and catch up with them later. With Tom and Jackie already committed to the sea trial, despite their reservations about being on the boat with only the three men, they trusted the De Leons and proceeded with the plan.

Tom took the helm of the boat, navigating them towards open water. Once they were far from the dock and any land, an unexpected development occurred. Skyler and John approached Tom, informing him that they wanted to show him something in the lower levels of the vessel. Curious, Tom accompanied them below deck to the bedroom area. Meanwhile, Alonzo and Jackie were positioned in the kitchen area directly above the bedroom.

It was in this moment that a loud and chaotic disturbance erupted from the bedroom. Alonzo, recognizing the noise, knew it signaled the attack on Tom by Skyler and John. Reacting swiftly, Alonzo moved towards Jackie, taking hold of her. Before she could comprehend the situation, Alonzo forcefully pushed her to the ground, secured her hands behind her back, and produced handcuffs to restrain her.

Jackie was brought into the bedroom, where she confronted the sight of her husband, Tom. He lay on the bed, handcuffed and immobilized. Jackie herself was thrown onto the bed beside him. In this dire situation, Jackie looked at Skyler, pleading for answers. She mentioned how they had met his wife and held their baby. She implored them to let them return to land and be with their family. However, Skyler remained indifferent to her pleas. He instructed Alonzo to tape their mouths and eyes.

As Skyler took control of the boat's

navigation, piloting it toward the deepest part of the ocean, Alonzo and John remained in the bedroom with Tom and Jackie. Tom, despite his restraints, managed to console Jackie, stroking her hand and reassuring her that they would face whatever came next together. The boat eventually halted, having reached its destination at the ocean's depths. Skyler ordered Alonzo and John to bring Tom and Jackie onto the deck.

Out on the deck, Skyler forced Tom and Jackie to sign the sale documents for the boat. Additionally, he coerced them into signing paperwork that granted him access to their bank accounts. During this unsettling process, Jackie intentionally misspelled her last name on one of the signature blocks, a deliberate act to signal that she was signing under duress.

With the documents signed, the group moved to the back of the boat. Skyler instructed Alonzo to retrieve the anchor from the front. Realizing the gravity of their situation, Jackie pleaded with the men to spare their lives, to allow them to return to their family. Tom managed to free himself from John's grasp and delivered a powerful kick to Skyler's groin. Despite this resistance, John subdued both Tom and Jackie.

Bound back-to-back with their handcuffs interlinked, Tom and Jackie sat on the deck, helpless. Alonzo approached, dragging the heavy anchor with him. Positioned adjacent to Tom and Jackie, the anchor lay beside them. Skyler then connected the end of a long metal chain from the anchor to their handcuffs. Ensuring their restraints were securely attached to the chain, Skyler lifted the anchor and hurled it overboard.

As the anchor plunged into the water, Tom and Jackie would have been subjected to a sequence of terrifying sensations. The initial moments would be dominated by the cacophonous sound of the chain being pulled off the boat and plunging into the water below. The chain's links would have scraped and grinded over the wooden railing as it rapidly unraveled. With each link sliding over the railing, the chain would become increasingly taut until it yanked Tom and Jackie towards the side of the vessel.

Alonzo later recounted that during this pivotal moment, the force of the anchor pulled Jackie's head against the inner side of the boat with a resounding, audible crack. This impact marked the beginning of the horrifying ordeal that awaited them. As the chain tensioned, Tom and Jackie would have found themselves in a desperate struggle against the anchor's weight, as it aimed to pull them off the boat and into the water.

In this moment of despair, Skyler, Alonzo, and John merely observed, showing no intention of intervening or offering any aid. Tom attempted to grasp onto anything within reach, attempting to hold on to his wife and defy the force of the anchor. Despite his efforts, the combined weight of the anchor and the boat's movement proved insurmountable. Slowly but inexorably, Tom and Jackie were drawn upwards and over the boat's railing, until they were plunged into the water.

Upon entering the water, Tom and Jackie would have been acutely conscious, experiencing the chilling reality of their predicament. Fully aware, they would have embarked on a harrowing descent into the abyss, plummeting toward the ocean floor situated 3,500 feet below.

The aftermath of the crime was equally disturbing. Jennifer, far from being an innocent bystander, was an active participant in the scheme. Her calculated manipulation had lured Tom and Jackie into the deadly trap. Skyler's reports to Jennifer throughout the crime exposed the extent of their malevolent partnership. Even after the murder, Jennifer and Skyler shamelessly utilized the Hawks' video camera, erasing the memories of the victims and using the camera to document their own lives.

Despite his cooperation, Alonso was sentenced to 20 years in prison, a concession for his role in the crime. Jennifer, the mastermind behind the plot, faced a life sentence without the possibility of parole, reflecting the gravity of her involvement. Skyler and John Kennedy, the architects of the brutal act, received the harshest penalty – the death sentence.

"Trapped Beneath: The Unthinkable Ordeal of the Pointe-à-Pierre Divers."

On February 25, 2022, Christopher Boodram, a 36-year-old father of three, began his day in his modest Pointe-à-Pierre home on the Caribbean Island of Trinidad and Tobago. Being careful not to disturb his still-sleeping wife, he quietly left his bed and proceeded to another room for his customary morning exercise routine. Once his exercises were done, he moved to the kitchen to prepare breakfast. By 5:30 a.m., Christopher was stepping out of his front door, ready for his daily commute to work.

Christopher's career as a professional scuba diver had extended for more than ten years. His expertise had carved a niche in the domain of commercial diving, encompassing a diverse array of tasks carried out underwater. These tasks spanned from inspections and welding to the relocation of equipment. Fortunes had favored Christopher for the past eight months, placing him with a company conveniently situated just two minutes away from his home. This company was none other than Paria Fuel, an oil and gas enterprise. Within Paria Fuel, Christopher played a crucial role in the maintenance and protection of multiple underwater pipelines that facilitated the transfer of oil from ships to land. These pipelines, totaling a minimum of six, held a unique U-shaped design. Each pipeline featured vertical segments that rose above the water's surface and connected via a horizontal 1200-foot section of pipe situated approximately 60 feet beneath the water's surface.

One of these vertical segments extended into the open sea, roughly 1200 feet away from the coastline.

Vessels sailing by would utilize this opening to deposit their cargo of oil. The oil would travel down the pipe, traverse the horizontal expanse, and ascend the other vertical segment situated nearer to the shore. At this juncture, workers would collect the oil, initiating its transition from sea to land for subsequent processing.

It was an ordinary day in February when Christopher arrived at Paria Fuel, greeted by the anticipated news that he and his fellow divers would be undertaking maintenance on one of these underwater pipelines. However, a unique aspect set this particular assignment apart. The pipeline, referred to as birth number six, stood distinct from Paria Fuel's operational oil transport conduits. Birth number six had remained inactive since 2018, a four-year period that saw it being purposefully kept dormant. The vertical portion of the pipeline extending into the sea retained its original form, protruding above the water's surface. In contrast, the adjacent vertical section closer to the shore underwent a deliberate alteration. This segment had been sealed using an expansive inflatable plug, akin to a massive pool toy placed within the pipe. This inflatable stopper, upon inflation, created a watertight seal, making the section impervious to water. Consequently, this section was submerged underwater, positioned around five to ten feet beneath the water's surface. This strategic submersion aimed to prevent interference with ships navigating in proximity to the shore. Additionally, a structure known as a "habitat" was situated atop the opening of the submerged vertical segment of birth number six.

To better understand the concept of the habitat, imagine a situation in a bathtub. Visualize an empty bucket turned upside down and gradually lowered beneath the water's surface. As long as the bucket remains level and undisturbed, an air pocket is trapped within it. This air pocket ensures that the area beneath the bucket stays dry even when submerged in water. Similar to this principle, the habitat created a sealed chamber atop the submerged vertical segment of birth number six. It held a pocket of air, allowing for a dry enclave within the watery surroundings.

Paria Fuel executed an ingenious approach. They lowered a metaphorical colossal bucket into the water and secured it directly above the entrance of the submerged vertical segment. This shrewd maneuver created a lasting air pocket, encapsulating the pipe's opening. This unique arrangement served a crucial purpose. Whenever maintenance was required on this pipeline—such as the task Christopher and his colleagues were about to undertake—divers could descend to the habitat. Positioned within the habitat, they would stand on a small metal platform, shedding their unwieldy diving apparatus to work on the pipe while breathing air. This provision presented an unparalleled convenience.

After receiving instructions about reactivating birth number six, Christopher and his fellow divers efficiently organized their equipment and assigned responsibilities for their upcoming task. The plan outlined the work they would undertake once submerged within the habitat. The divers formed a tight-knit unit, their bond forged through numerous shared undertakings. Christopher's companions included Kazim Ali Jr,

Yusuf Henry, Fyzal Kerban, and Rishi Nagassar. These men had collaborated on multiple occasions, fostering not only a professional relationship but also a friendship that extended beyond the workplace.

As their boat positioned itself just off the coastline, anchoring above the submerged birth number six pipe, the divers began their descent. Skillfully navigating around the habitat's perimeter, they entered the breathable air pocket, which allowed them access to the pipe's entrance. Finding footing on the platform inside, they removed their bulky diving equipment and proceeded with their task while wearing wetsuits.

The mission's goal appeared straightforward: activate a lever inside the pipe to deflate the substantial inflatable plug that sealed it. However, a complication arose—when one of the divers tried to operate the lever, it resisted movement. The solution involved obtaining a wrench to loosen the stubborn lever. The responsibility of retrieving the necessary tool fell to Kazim, who volunteered to ascend to the surface.

Kazim geared up for his ascent from beneath the habitat, resurfacing to communicate with the boat's crew and retrieve the needed wrench. After obtaining the tool, he returned to the habitat, presenting the wrench to his fellow divers to tackle the challenge at hand.

With steadfast concentration, the diver armed with the wrench repositioned himself, resolute as he inserted the tool and maneuvered the lever. His persistence paid off as the lever finally gave way, overcoming its resistance. Yet, the instant the lever was activated, an utterly harrowing event unfolded within the confined space of that habitat.

The sequence of events that unfolded, as well as the potential preventive measures that could have been taken, remain elusive. When the lever was set in motion, a chain reaction was initiated. This lever's movement led to the deflation of the plug that had sealed the dormant pipeline for four years. This breach in the seal created an abrupt transition between the low-pressure air within the 1,200-foot pipeline and the high-pressure air within the habitat. As per the laws of physics, air always moves from areas of higher pressure to those of lower pressure. Consequently, as the seal was compromised, the high-pressure air from the habitat surged into the pipe below. This swift process transformed the pipe's opening into a vacuum, all within a fraction of a second. The abrupt pressure differential triggered an involuntary suction force, forcefully pulling the entire contents of the habitat—along with the divers and their equipment—into the pipe's opening. The forceful entry of seawater into the pipe further underscored the rapid and unyielding nature of this disaster.

Deprived of their scuba gear, the five men experienced a rapid and remarkable transformation. Their static stance outside the pipe gave way to a frantic flight into its depths, propelled by the unrelenting pull of the vacuum. As water enveloped them, pressure equalized, and their trajectory came to an abrupt stop within a slightly elevated section of the horizontal pipeline. In this space, a narrow pocket of air allowed them to gasp for the precious oxygen that had eluded them for an agonizing period.

In the ensuing moments,

communication became a frenzied exchange of reassurance and mutual acknowledgment of their survival. Amidst the pitch-black abyss, their voices connected, reaffirming their presence and shared experience. The awareness that they had emerged from this ordeal, though battered, instilled a renewed determination within them. Amid the cacophony of voices reverberating up and down the pipeline, their combined efforts started to bring clarity to their dire predicament. Assessing their spatial orientation, they collectively decided that Christopher, positioned closest to the pipe's entrance, should lead their attempt to escape. With a shared sense of purpose, they devised a plan for the journey back, a journey that, against all odds, held the potential to lead them to safety.

Urging his companions to remain composed, Christopher orchestrated a strategic formation where each diver's feet were linked to the one below, shoulders forming the crucial link in this human chain. The propulsion method within the confined space was as rudimentary as it was effective: they pressed their heels against the walls, inching forward in a slow, deliberate motion. This painstaking progression, while excruciatingly slow, carried with it a glimmer of hope. Despite the agony pulsating through their battered bodies and the thinning thread of their endurance, they navigated this suffocating conduit, retracing the path they had unwittingly journeyed.

As their journey began, Christopher quickly encountered the initial flooded section of the pipe. The length of this submerged portion was a mystery, adding to the uncertainty they faced. Venturing into the underwater passage, they realized that their options were limited—either they would discover another air pocket or face the risk of drowning.

In this critical moment, it became evident that only Christopher and Fyzal were willing and physically capable of attempting this dangerous task. The gravity of their situation fueled panic among the others who were not part of this daring attempt. Their pleas echoed as they begged Christopher and Fyzal not to abandon them.

Feeling an intense sense of responsibility, Christopher and Fyzal were resolute that someone needed to reach the surface and seek help. With their resolve firm, the two men linked together and cautiously entered the dark flooded section of the pipe. Suspended in pitch-black uncertainty, they ventured underwater, using breath holds to propel themselves gradually forward. Miraculously, the initial submerged section they encountered turned out to be relatively short. Overcoming fits of coughing and gagging, they emerged on the other side into another air pocket.

In a remarkable turn of events, Christopher located two air tanks above him in the new air pocket. Passing one tank down to Fyzal, this discovery offered a lifeline, providing both men with an air supply that could sustain them during the longer submerged sections of the pipe. With the heavy tanks positioned on their heads, they pressed on. Navigating through successive flooded sections, Christopher and Fyzal remained resolute, their determination unwavering.

Hours of tense and terrifying struggle ensued. Christopher and Faisal pressed on, grappling with their dwindling air reserves and the fear of the unknown. They advanced through these harrowing stretches, enduring the mental and physical strain of their predicament. Finally, after countless flooded sections, Fyzal's state of mind began to deteriorate. In the darkness, he shouted for Christopher to halt, his fear palpable. Christopher sensed Fyzal's distress, even without visual confirmation, as the two men grappled with the overwhelming challenges of their ordeal.

Christopher remained composed, trying to calm Fyzal and convince him to join him. However, as Fyzal's panic persisted, Christopher made the difficult decision to continue on alone, promising to return with help. Despite Fyzal's pleas for him to stop, Christopher knew he had to press forward. With the sound of his friend's cries echoing in his ears, Christopher clenched the mouthpiece between his teeth, pushing the air tank above his head, and slowly inched his way towards the entrance of the pipe.

Navigating through a long underwater section, Christopher's air was running out. Just as he reached the point where the pipe turned vertical, he knew that the habitat was above him.

Summoning his remaining strength, Christopher turned and swam up the vertical section until he emerged into yet another air pocket. However, this time, the water level was not close enough to the exit of the pipe for him to pull himself out. Stuck at the bottom of the vertical section, Christopher faced a seemingly insurmountable obstacle.

Fortunately, a dangling chain within arm's reach provided a lifeline for Christopher. He grabbed onto it, holding on as he waited for help, unsure if anyone was coming to rescue them. Eventually, two rescue divers reached the habitat and pulled Christopher out of the pipe, saving his life. As he emerged, Christopher witnessed the presence of the Paria Fuel Emergency Response Team and the Trinidad and Tobago Coast Guard on the scene, preparing for a rescue operation.

Despite his trauma and injuries, Christopher rushed to the authorities and informed them that his four colleagues were still alive, trapped in air pockets within the pipe. He could hear their banging and pleas for help. He implored the authorities to go back down and save them. Regrettably, the decision was made that it was too dangerous to send rescuers into the pipe.

After his own rescue, Christopher attempted to check himself out of the hospital's Intensive Care Unit to go back and rescue his friends, but he was prevented from doing so. Over the course of two agonizing days, his colleagues remained trapped inside the pipe, their banging and noises audible from the surface. Tragically, by February 27th, the noises ceased, indicating that all of the trapped men had lost their lives. The exact causes of each of their deaths were multifaceted—some may have succumbed to suffocation due to the lack of air, others to injuries sustained during the ordeal, and a possibility exists that some attempted to navigate the underwater sections without scuba tanks, resulting in drowning. The recovery process unfolded over time: the bodies of three divers were retrieved on February 28th, and the final body was discovered on March 3rd.

It's puzzling why Christopher and the other divers didn't take steps to balance the pressure inside the habitat and the pipe before removing the plug. This vacuum effect, called Delta p, could have been expected and prevented with relative ease. The investigation into the exact chain of events and who's at fault is still ongoing. However, Christopher, the only survivor, and many others believe that Paria Fuel holds significant responsibility for not initiating a rescue operation during the first two days when the trapped divers' banging on the pipe was clearly audible.

Thanks for Reading!

We hope that you found these stories to be as disturbing and thought-provoking as we did.

These stories are a reminder of the dark side of human nature. They show depths of depravity that people can sink to, and the suffering that can be inflicted on others.

But these stories are also a reminder of the human spirit. They show us how people can overcome even the most difficult of challenges, and how hope can still be found in the darkest of times.

We hope that you will take these stories with you and think about them long after you have finished reading this book. We hope that they will make you think about the world around you in a new way, and that they will inspire you to make a difference.

Printed in Great Britain
by Amazon